P9-DEP-279

The
CHRISTMAS
SINGING

Books by Cindy Woodsmall

The CHRISTMAS SINGING

A Romance from the Heart of Amish Country

CINDY WOODSMALL

WATERBROOK
PRESS

THE CHRISTMAS SINGING
PUBLISHED BY WATERBROOK PRESS
12265 Oracle Boulevard, Suite 200
Colorado Springs, Colorado 80921

The characters and events in this book are fictional, and any resemblance to actual persons or events is coincidental.

ISBN 978-0-307-44654-1
ISBN 978-0-307-45921-3 (electronic)

Copyright © 2011 by Cindy Woodsmall

Cover design by Mark D. Ford; cover photo of snowy street scene by Dale Yoder; author photo by Tammy Miller, Light Photography

All rights reserved. No part of this book may be reproduced or transmitted in any form or by any means, electronic or mechanical, including photocopying and recording, or by any information storage and retrieval system, without permission in writing from the publisher.

Published in the United States by WaterBrook Multnomah, an imprint of the Crown Publishing Group, a division of Random House Inc., New York.

WATERBROOK and its deer colophon are registered trademarks of Random House Inc.

Printed in the United States of America
2011—First Edition

10 9 8 7 6 5 4 3 2 1

To Shannon Marchese, my editor and friend

With each book the road before us unfolds
with a few sharp turns and jolting potholes,
but whatever challenges arise,
you remain on my top-ten list of people
I'm thankful to have in my life.
Even though you're a new mom
and my first grandchild is on her way,
time and again you give wise counsel I can depend on.
Sometimes in life we know a relationship was meant to be,
and we are one of those.

You surprise me, challenge me, encourage me, bail me out,
and on an occasion or two, you've driven me nuts—
and I couldn't be more grateful.

One

Cold darkness and the sugary aroma from the cake shop below surrounded Mattie as she slid a solid-colored dress over her head and tied her white apron in place. The Old Order Amish here in Ohio didn't wear the black aprons—a difference she enjoyed—and only those involved with baking wore the white apron from the waist down. After brushing her hair, she fastened it up properly and donned her prayer *Kapp*. Who needed a light or a mirror to get ready for the day? She'd been wearing similar clothes her whole life, and the Ohio Amish pinned up their hair in much the same way as she had back in Pennsylvania.

Now, cake decorating—that required good lighting and great attention to detail. And her favorite season for making specialty cakes—Christmas—was right around the corner.

Ready to take on a new day, she hurried down the rough-hewn steps that led into her shop, lit a kerosene lantern, and pulled on her coat while going out the back door. Before getting to the woodpile, she paused a moment, enjoying Berlin's lights. Illuminated white bulbs hung like beacons against the dark night. Although she missed her *Mamm* and *Daed,* this was home now, not Pennsylvania.

She scanned the silhouettes and shadows of nearby homes and shops. The golden full moon had a silky glow around it, a ring almost as clear and defined as the moon itself. What would it look like if she designed a cake with a halo?

Eager to make notes, she loaded wood into the crook of her arm and went inside. She dumped the logs in the bin and then stirred the embers in the potbelly stove and added kindling. Before her first customer arrived, she'd have the place toasty warm.

The shop was old and narrow, but Mattie loved it. When the previous owner, a man who sold saddles and such, decided to sell his place a few weeks before she moved here, her brother James had helped her buy and remodel it. They'd torn out all the old counters, workbenches, and shelving.

The ceiling, floors, and walls were made of unfinished, exposed wood. She'd put in a huge display case along the left wall, and a couple of small tables sat to the right. Stainless-steel sinks and a gas-powered commercial oven and refrigerator filled the back wall. Her work station, where she pieced together and decorated her cakes, sat a few feet away. Even in cooler weather, keeping the place warm without electricity wasn't much of an issue with the heat radiating from the oven and the wood stove. Hot summer weather was a little more problematic, but the many windows helped.

She began searching for her spiral notebook, which she often referred to as her brain. The pages of her combination sketch pad, scrapbook, and journal were covered with drawings, doodles, and pictures from magazines and newspapers. It'd been a gift for her twelfth birthday, and although the gift giver had broken her heart seven years later, she still appreciated the book. Her day planner was in the back of it, with the types of cakes she needed to make, due dates, and all her clients' names and phone numbers. Without it she wouldn't know how to run her store.

She knelt and looked under her work station. It was there, maybe two feet away. Reaching as far as she could, she touched the edge of the thick binder and grabbed it. Now where did she leave her pencil?

Is it behind your ear, Mattie Lane? Gideon's voice washed over her.

She shuddered, detesting hearing him inside her head, especially with the added use of the pet name *Mattie Lane. Lane* was not a part of her given name or her surname. When they first broke up, his voice had played constantly in her mind, but after three years these whispers from the past were rare.

They'd been good friends most of their lives. He was three years older than she, and it had stung when he began dating at sixteen. But worse than seeing him with other Amish girls was seeing him with *Englischer* girls. At eighteen, he'd stopped seeing others and told her that he'd decided to wait for her.

Their first date had taken place on her birthday, Christmas Eve, and she'd attended her first singing with Gideon. The magic of Christmas seemed to surround both of them as their voices rose in celebration of Christ's birth and the blessing of being together. Nothing in her life had ever compared to the emotion of that night, not even owning her own shop. For the next three years, they enjoyed the glorious Christmas singings together.

And then she caught him.

Her heartbreak had been compounded by confusion. *Nothing* had prepared her for his betrayal.

Pushing those thoughts away, she found a pencil lying next to the sink and jotted down notes about the halo. Then she made herself a quick breakfast. Before she'd swallowed the last of her coffee, she had four dozen muffins and four dozen cupcakes in the oven.

The cowbells hanging on the door chimed numerous times throughout the morning, and by noon she had sold the usual amount of baked goods for this time of year and had taken three new cake orders—for a birthday, a bridal shower, and a summer wedding. She couldn't think of anything more exciting than running Mattie Cakes.

She went to the phone and dialed her Mamm. One of the things she loved most about owning a shop was the permission to have a phone handy. She called her Mamm at least once a day.

Few women were as remarkable as her mother. She'd been forty-seven when she got pregnant with Mattie. But Mamm's health issues progressed from inconvenient at the time of Mattie's birth to life threatening by the time Mattie turned sixteen. Mattie had spent much of her life fearing she'd lose her mother. But when Mattie hesitated to move from Pennsylvania to Ohio, her mother had refused to let her stay in Apple Ridge.

After ten rings the answering machine clicked on. Since Mamm was seventy and her phone was in the shanty near the barn, Mattie rarely reached her on the first try of the day.

At the beep, Mattie said, "Good morning, Mamm and Daed. This is your adoring, favorite daughter calling." Mattie chuckled. "Being the only girl has perks… Anyway, I'm having a great day, and I want to hear about yours. I'll call back at two thirty. I hope you're dressed warmly. Love you both." If Mattie established a time she'd call back, Mamm never failed to be in the phone shanty, waiting to hear from her. Daed had set up a comfortable chair and a gas heater out there. She talked to her Daed too, but he didn't stay on the line long.

The bells on the shop door jingled again, and a cold blast of November air burst into the room.

Mattie's almost-five-year-old niece came barreling through the door, bundled up in her black winter coat and a wool scarf over her prayer Kapp. Mattie wondered if Esther had walked the half block from her house to the shop by herself or if the little girl's mother was trailing behind, pushing her two youngest children in a double stroller. Esther also had four older siblings, but all of them were in school during the day.

"Mattie Cakes!" the young girl cried.

Mattie chuckled at Esther's excitement. None of her nieces or nephews called her "Aunt Mattie" these days, but she found this nickname adorable.

Esther ran to her, clutching a silver lunch pail. "You didn't come home to eat, so I brought you some food."

"Denki." Mattie wasn't surprised when Esther held on to the pail. Her niece loved toting things.

Esther began her routine inspection of the store, beginning with the sink full of dirty cooking utensils. She enjoyed coming to the shop, and Mattie hoped that in seven or eight years, Esther might want to learn the trade. Esther's older sisters didn't seem to have any desire to make cakes.

Sol walked in, carrying a bow, a quiver full of arrows, and his camouflage duffel bag. He set it all behind her work counter, looking more confident than he used to. "Hi." He flashed a quick smile before looking down. Sometimes shy, he didn't keep eye contact for long.

They'd begun seeing each other on special occasions more than two years ago. Now they saw each other regularly, and unlike Gideon, Sol found getting along with young women a challenge. He was reserved and tended to mumble, but Mattie and Sol liked being together.

When the bell on the door jingled again but no one came in, Sol hurried to open it for Mattie's sister-in-law as she pushed the stroller into the room.

"Did you forget something, Mattie?" Dorothy asked. "Like coming home for lunch?"

Mattie glanced at the clock. "Sorry. I didn't realize how much time had passed."

Dorothy sighed. "I've heard that before."

"And you'll hear it again," Sol mumbled. A grin sneaked across his face as he stole a glance at Mattie. She wanted to hug him, but he liked to keep his distance before a hunt. He didn't bathe or shave for a day or two before leaving, not wanting to scare off the wild game by smelling of soap or aftershave.

Mattie held out her hands for the pail. "Thank you very

much, Esther. If your Mamm doesn't mind, I think you should pick out a cupcake."

Esther gave her the pail and gazed up at her mother.

Dorothy hesitated, probably calculating all sorts of mom things—like how many sweets Esther had eaten this week, if she'd had her fruits and vegetables today, and if Mattie was spoiling her. "Oh, all right."

Esther clapped and hurried to the display case housing the decorated cupcakes. "You made turkey cakes!" Each one had a tiny turkey head made of marzipan and tail feathers of icing.

"*Ya,* I did."

Dorothy stood near Mattie's work station and craned to see the display case. "You made so many."

"It's Thanksgiving next week. People have placed orders for most of those and will pick them up late this afternoon. I'll make even more for tomorrow's orders. The Englischer girls and boys have class parties before they're out for the holiday next week. This year I've gone an extra step. The feathers are not only a different color from the frosting, but they have a mildly different flavor too." Mattie opened the wood stove and stoked it before adding another piece of wood. "I think it's some of my best blending of colors and tastes yet…for cupcakes designed to look like turkeys."

Dorothy set the brake on the stroller and moved to a stool. "I still don't understand why you go to that much trouble for something that will be devoured in less than two minutes."

"Only the cake is gone. The memory will last much longer, perhaps days or a month or a lifetime. Just look at Esther."

The four-year-old was talking to herself, or to the cakes, as she tried to choose one.

Dorothy's face eased into a smile. "I guess I do understand. You know, come to think of it, James and I still talk about the ten-year anniversary cake you made for us." Dorothy sighed. "But we want to see you more. You sleep here and skip meals. At least hang the Out to Lunch sign and come eat with us."

Sol pulled a flashlight out of his bag and made sure it was working before taking a seat on his usual stool at the far end of her work station. "Would you feel better if she gave her word that she'd try to come home for lunch from now on?"

Dorothy laughed. "Ya, it would make me feel better...even though I know it won't change a thing."

Mattie held up her hand as if taking an oath. "I will do my best not to lose track of time and to follow all your advice."

"Wait until you have little ones and are trying to herd them toward the table," Dorothy teased.

Sol winked at Mattie. They were in agreement on this topic—they'd definitely marry one day, but it'd be a while.

Dorothy turned to her. "So what has you so preoccupied this time?"

Mattie grabbed her notepad. "Look at this." She opened the spiral-bound book and tapped the rough sketch of her halo cake. "Wouldn't this be an unusual wedding cake?"

Dorothy leaned in, wearing a slight frown. "I suppose if I were an Englischer, it'd snag my interest. Is that a net? Is it edible?"

"Oh, ya. And it's not a net. It's a halo...of sorts."

"How on earth will you get it to surround a cake in midair like that?"

Mattie splayed her fingers and waved her hands over the notebook. "I can do magic."

Dorothy chuckled. "Ya, magic that takes weeks of hard work."

A car horn tooted. Sol stood. "That's my ride."

"What zone are you headed for?" Mattie put several cupcakes in a bakery box.

"C." He shoved his flashlight into his duffel bag.

She was sure he'd told her the zone before, but she didn't try to keep his hunting schedule straight any more than he tried to keep up with the type of cake she needed to bake next.

He slung the bow and quiver over one shoulder and his duffel bag over the other. "We're going to a campsite in Hocking Hills. I have several tags, so I hope to bring back a few deer."

"The venison will come in handy this winter at the soup kitchen." She passed him the box of goodies.

"Denki." He studied her for a moment, grinning. "Don't get into any trouble while I'm gone."

It was his way of telling her that he cared. "I won't."

He opened the door. "See you in a few days."

"I'll be here." Mattie returned to her open scrapbook, wondering if she could fashion the framework for the halo out of hardened sugar.

Dorothy sighed. "Isn't there a limit on how much wild game the local charities will accept? Sol told James that he's going on a seven-day hunt less than a week after Thanksgiving."

"Ya. He is." Mattie pointed at her chicken scratch of a sketch. "I think I know how to make the halo. What if I made an edible dowel from my crispy rice concoction and anchored—"

"Something's wrong." Dorothy cut her off.

"With the halo idea?"

"No." Her sister-in-law placed her hand on the notebook. "I know Sol builds pallets from his parents' house, but even so, how does he manage to get off work so much?"

"As long as he meets his quota each week, he can spend

the rest of his time doing whatever he wants. He works long hours some days so he can take off when he wants. Is that a problem?"

"No…" Dorothy turned pages in the book without looking at it. "Honey, everyone in the family likes Sol. But…"

Mattie folded her arms, ready to defend herself. With seven big brothers, she knew how to stand her ground. "But what?"

"I keep waiting to see in you the zest that young people in love always have. It seems there's no more now than when you started courting two years ago. Am I wrong?"

Mattie shrugged, hoping to keep the conversation short. "Sol has all the traits I could want in a husband. Zest isn't on the list."

Dorothy leaned in. "When you love someone enough to marry him, you find him fascinating. You love being in the same room with him. You desire to bear his children. You have a bond that's so powerful you'll gladly overlook the things about him that will drive you crazy years later."

"What Sol and I have doesn't fit that description, but our bond is strong. Maybe letting each other pursue outside interests is more important than you think."

"He's not one of your brothers, Mattie. After fourteen years James and I still arrange our days to get as much time together as possible." She looked up at Mattie. "He draws me, Mattie, and I, him. People in love should have that."

Mattie once had that kind of relationship with Gideon, and Dorothy knew it. What she didn't understand was that Mattie and Sol's relationship was much better, at least for her. "Dorothy, I know you want the best thing for me, but you have to trust me. Sol and I are very happy."

Dorothy nodded, not looking convinced, but Mattie wasn't bothered by what she or the rest of the family thought. She knew what being with Sol meant.

The bell jingled, and more cold air rushed inside along with Willa Carter and her son. Excitement danced inside Mattie. The whole time she'd worked on Ryan's birthday cake, she looked forward to seeing his eyes light up when he saw it.

"Happy birthday, Ryan." She closed her notebook and set it aside.

"Mattie!" Dorothy lifted it off the wood stove. "Think… please."

"Oh, yes. Thanks." She thought in English and used it easily these days, a result of having regular contact with her non-Amish customers and friends. She turned to the little boy. He was so cute in his blue jeans and cowboy hat. "How old are you today?"

Ryan held up four fingers. "I'm this many!"

Mattie stepped out from behind the counter. "You are so big!" She turned to Mrs. Carter, who was jamming her car keys into her bright red purse. "How are you today?"

"Frazzled." She unbuttoned her plaid coat. "I forgot this place sat so far back from the other stores, and I parked halfway down the block."

Dorothy shifted her stroller out of the center of the floor. "We'd better go."

Mattie grabbed a small dessert box and moved to the case of cupcakes, where her niece stood. "Did you decide which one you want?"

Esther pointed one out, and Mattie boxed it up. "Here you go."

"You eat the lunch we brought," Dorothy whispered.

"Okay." Mattie mocked a loud whisper in return.

Esther shook her little forefinger at Mattie. "I'm comin' back to check after I have my cupcake and milk."

"You do that." Mattie held the door for them before returning her attention to Ryan. "Come." She went to the refrigerator, and as she removed the plastic cover from the cake, the smell of chocolate wafted out. She carried the cake over to Ryan.

Ryan gasped. "Mommy, look!"

A smiling teddy bear stared up at them. The three-dimensional bear had come out just as she'd hoped, and the look in Ryan's eyes made every hour of effort worth it. This wasn't her first time to create a bear cake, but she'd used the new specialty tips that had arrived earlier in the week, and the results looked even better than she'd imagined. The bear's claws, paws, and facial features nearly jumped out of the box.

"It's perfect, Mattie." Mrs. Carter's smile reflected appreciation. "When my girlfriend told me about your shop, I never expected such excellent work."

The pleasure of this moment would linger with Mattie for a long time. "Thank you."

"I have a daughter turning thirteen next month. She ice-skates, does ballet, and plays basketball. Think you could design a cake around one of her activities?"

"Sure." Mattie grabbed her scrapbook and flipped it open. "Or I could do one that showcases all three." She showed her several pages.

Mrs. Carter pointed at a triple-tier cake. "That one."

"I can put a different sport on each tier."

"She'll love that!" Mrs. Carter turned away quickly, scooping up Ryan, who had begun to race around the small store.

Mattie jotted down a few notes, feeling exuberant, then set the book aside. "I'll call you next week, and we'll make specific plans. Let me help you with this cake." Since Mrs. Carter was parked so far away, Mattie moved Ryan's cake to a stainless steel utility cart and grabbed her coat.

Mrs. Carter secured the squirming boy in one arm and pulled out a check she'd already written.

Without glancing at it, Mattie slid it into her coat pocket and wheeled the cart toward the front of the store.

"I hate asking you to leave the store unattended, but he is so wound up."

"I don't have anything baking in the oven, so it'll be fine."

Sol sat in the front passenger seat, half listening to the conversation between Amish Henry, his brother Daniel, and the driver, Eric. All were a little younger than he and eager to be on this trip.

Eric turned down the radio. "So my neighbor, the one with two hundred acres who hasn't let anyone hunt on it for more than thirty years…"

That caught Sol's attention. "Thirty years?"

"Yeah, he's always been real picky about who he lets on his property, but he said we could hunt it. Says the deer have really been ripping up his cornfields the last few years."

"Let's do it!" Amish Henry said.

"There's a catch," Eric said. "His mother is elderly and doesn't want to hear gunshots or have hunters stomping around on the land, so we'd be limited to Christmas Eve and Day, because they'll be away visiting relatives then."

Reality overtook Sol's moment of excitement. "I'm out. I can't go on Christmas Eve. That's Mattie's birthday, and she's got a thing about us attending the Christmas singing."

"Must be nice to have a girl," Daniel said. "I might give up hunting altogether if I had one."

"Not hunt at all?" Sol laughed. "If that's what she wants, you've got the wrong girl."

Eric clicked on the turn signal. "Why don't you hunt just in the morning on Christmas Eve and Christmas Day? You could probably tag your quota and still be back before noon. Come on, man. It'll be great."

"Ya, maybe." Sol tapped the dessert box that held the cupcakes. "I want to talk to Mattie before I agree to anything."

Eric pulled into the parking lot of a fish-and-wildlife store. "I need to get a few things."

They all piled out with him. Sol didn't need anything, but it never hurt to look around. He went to the knife case to see if they had anything new.

"Can I show you a particular knife?" the man behind the counter asked.

"Nah, I'm just looking. Thanks."

A girl stopped beside him, and his peripheral vision told him she was Amish. She pointed at various knives. "He'd like one of every kind he doesn't already have." He recognized the voice. Katie King.

Sol's insides knotted, and he stepped away from her. Their eyes met, and she smiled. She had dark hair and even darker eyes. He'd always thought she was pretty. But looks weren't what mattered to him. It was the way two people fit into each other's lives that really meant something.

His gut twisted with nerves, and he wished she'd leave. Mattie had never once made him uncomfortable, even when they first talked after the singings. She was the one who had approached him each time, but she did it in a reserved way—not staring or saying anything that he didn't know how to respond to. He'd never asked to take a girl home from a singing. Mattie, in her quiet, self-assured way, had asked him.

Katie put one hand on her hip. "I sure see you out with your friends a lot. I guess you shy guys have to stick together. It's a shame though, ya?"

Sol shrugged, not at all sure what answer she was fishing for. He never knew how to carry on a conversation with someone like Katie—all bubbly and blabbering about nothing at all. Mattie said what needed to be said and talked about things that made sense.

Amish Henry stepped out from an aisle, looking as if he wanted to rescue Sol but wasn't sure how. "You about ready?"

"Ya." Sol nodded. "Bye." He started to leave.

Katie stepped in front of him. "I think it'd be neat to climb a tree stand in the early morning hours and wait for dawn."

Sol wished Mattie would suddenly appear. He didn't understand women at all. Was Katie just being silly? He took another step back, studying her shoes, which were half covered in mud.

Katie angled her head, catching Sol's eye. "I hope you have a good trip." She turned and walked off.

Sol drew a deep breath, wondering if he'd ever get over some people making him feel as if he had a ten-pound block of ice in his gut.

Amish Henry adjusted his black felt hat. "I think she was hoping you'd ask her for a date."

The words jolted Sol. Her small talk and mannerisms made no sense to him, but maybe Amish Henry was right. He watched her leave. "Nah. She just wants to sit in somebody's tree stand."

"If that's what she wants from you, she'll never get it. Climbing into your tree stand? No way."

Sol laughed. "*Kumm* on. Let's find Daniel and Eric. We've got a long way to go before we can set up camp."

Two

*A*fter getting the cake into Mrs. Carter's vehicle and bidding her and her son good-bye, Mattie saw someone coming out of Today and Forever Books, where Mackenzie worked. They hadn't had a girl chat in weeks, and Mattie had been wanting time with her. She scurried toward the store, pushing the service cart along.

She parked the cart out front and stepped inside. Mackenzie stood behind the coffee shop counter, serving someone. She had on just enough makeup to give her color and wore a yellowish-gold sweater with a turkey on it.

Mackenzie glanced up, almost as if sensing she were there. "Hey!" Her friend's long, straight brown hair swayed as she came out from behind the counter and toward her. The store belonged to Mackenzie's grandfather, and as the current manager, she could take a break without asking anyone's permission. "Tell me you have time to visit over a whole pot of coffee."

Mattie hugged her. "I have time to visit over a pot of coffee."

"It's about time. I was going to come to Mattie Cakes when I caught a minute. We need to talk about the cake to celebrate our shop's thirtieth anniversary."

"Love the idea." Mattie slid out of her coat and tossed it over the back of a chair.

Mackenzie took a seat at the small round table. "Anyone scheduled to pick up an order today?"

"Not until almost closing time, and I've already finished preparing everything. But if you want to talk about my making something for the store's anniversary, I don't have my brain with me."

Mackenzie laughed. "I thought you never went anywhere without your notebook."

"Oh, I do…because I forget everything all the time. The day will come when I'll be working in the shop, a customer will walk in and give me a funny look, and I'll realize that I'm in my nightgown because I forgot to get dressed." Mattie laughed. "That's a real fear I have."

"Now I know what to get you for Christmas. I'll buy you a flannel nightgown. That way, if you do forget to get dressed, you'll look cute anyway."

"That's your best solution? That's just sad." Mattie tried to keep the grin off her face. "The answer is to come by my shop early, before any customers can arrive, and make sure I'm dressed."

"Before the sun's up? Sorry, but we're not that good of friends." Mackenzie's eyes lit up. "Okay...I'll loan you paper so we can talk about that cake I want."

Mackenzie stood and went into a back room.

The aroma of fresh-brewed coffee in the old wooden bookstore reminded Mattie of her shop, and the smell of books, both old and new, mixed together in a delightful scent.

Mattie looked at the coffee shop's display case, noticing how few muffins and cupcakes were left. Mackenzie's grandfather came by Mattie Cakes at nine thirty each morning and bought several dozen freshly made muffins and cupcakes. She made muffins only for herself and this store. Otherwise she was all about cakes.

Mackenzie sat down with paper, pen, two cups of coffee, and a basket holding cream, sugar, and stirrers. Mattie glanced at the clock.

"You need to get back?" Mackenzie asked.

"Not for a bit yet. When I called Mamm this morning, I left a message saying I'd call back at two thirty."

Mackenzie flipped her silky hair over her shoulder. "You say you forget everything, but I've never known you to forget to call your mom when you said you would."

Mattie poured a tiny cup of cream into her coffee before

stirring it. "Mamm means a lot to me, and with her health problems…I feel a need to stay connected. I always have. Plus, I appreciate her wisdom. When the time comes that she's not here, I can still rely on what she has taught me."

"I've never even thought about losing my mom. That seems morbid to me."

"My mom's seventy now, and her health's been delicate my whole life, so I've had to face the possibility of losing her."

"Isn't it emotionally exhausting to live as if she's going to die?"

"It's been a challenge to find a balance between caring and being burdened. But I think we've found it. The trick is not to let the power of what might happen tomorrow ruin today. She was diagnosed with lupus when I was sixteen, and she taught me how not to let her illness pull me under. But those lessons didn't come easily."

Mattie and Mackenzie talked for a long time, eventually discussing the type and size of cake Mattie needed to make as she took notes on loose-leaf paper. Mackenzie refilled their coffee mugs time and again. Mattie took another quick look at the clock and stood. "I need to go call Mamm now."

"You can use our phone."

Mattie went behind the counter and dialed her Mamm. Her mother picked up before the first ring finished.

"Mattie, sweetheart, is that you?"

"Ya, Mamm, it's me."

While she talked, a strange aroma caught her attention—chimney smoke, she guessed. Most of the nearby Englischer homes had fireplaces or wood stoves, but they were used more often in the evenings. The scent seemed strong. "Ya, Mamm, I'm coming home for Thanksgiving next week, and James and Dorothy want you and Daed to come for Christmas again this year."

"Is Sol coming with you for Thanksgiving?"

"I think he'll come this time. I'll know for sure in a few days."

Mackenzie slipped on her coat and went outside. Mattie continued talking with her Mamm, but she noticed a small group of shop owners standing outside without their coats. Some stared toward the sky. Others appeared to be talking intently.

Mamm wanted to know all about the cakes she'd been making and how she and Sol were doing, and most of all she wanted to be reminded over and over when they'd see each other again. "Next week, Mamm. I'll be there late Wednesday and stay until late Saturday."

Mackenzie tapped on the window, motioning for her.

"Mamm, I need to go." She'd barely gotten the words out of her mouth when her mother said good-bye and hung up. That was her Mamm. She loved to talk to Mattie, but she never wanted to hold her up if she needed to work.

Mackenzie stepped inside. "Mattie, there's smoke coming from somewhere down the block."

Concern charged through her. She put on her coat and gathered the scattered papers filled with diagrams and notes for the cake. When she stepped outside, she saw black smoke billowing from the direction of her shop.

Mattie's heart burned as if it were on fire. She ran down the sidewalk with Mackenzie right beside her. She turned the corner where her place sat off the main road. Flames licked the walls and roof.

"No!" Tears sprang to her eyes.

Mackenzie pushed numbers on her cell phone.

Through one of the first-floor windows, Mattie saw movement inside. A flash of burgundy caught her eye, reminding her of the dress her niece had on that morning.

"Esther!" Mattie threw down the papers she was carrying and took off running.

"Wait." Mackenzie grabbed her arm and stopped her. "You can't go in there."

Mattie jerked free and ran inside. "Esther!" She couldn't see anything but thick gray smoke. Turbulent flames lashed out but did nothing to light her way. "Esther!" Heat seared her dress, and her lungs burned. Wondering if Esther had tried to get away from the fire by going upstairs, Mattie dodged flames and embers and hurried to the second floor.

Three

The empty, almost-finished home echoed as Gideon built the doorjambs. Nothing felt as good as having the strength to work. It was something he never took for granted. Not anymore. Today he could hold a hammer and make a nail disappear into wood with little effort. But what about tomorrow?

He ignored the question and placed a level on one side of the closet doorframe, making sure the casing was aligned correctly. He struggled to keep the wood in place as he shifted from one tool to the next. Work on an oversized closet like this required two men, but the rest of the Beiler Construction team labored to get a new home dried in before winter. If snow or rain hit before the house was complete enough to keep the weather out, they'd have to replace damaged particle board, framing, and insulation, and all work might have to stop until spring.

His brother had promised Beth and Jonah, the owners of this house, that Gideon would be the one to complete it, including the punch list. He still had a ways to go on the job.

"Hello?" Jonah called.

"Master bedroom," Gideon answered.

Jonah's distinct tempo echoed through the unfinished place. He was only thirty, but as a teenager he had been injured in a sleigh ride accident that left him walking with a cane. "I came to lend a hand." Jonah already had on his tool belt. "I've cleared my schedule with the boss, and I have the rest of today and most of tomorrow to be your assistant."

"Good. I could use it."

Jonah was an artist by trade. He carved beautiful scenery into wood, bringing it to life, but he'd been a lead carpenter while building his previous home. And then he met the woman he lovingly referred to as "the boss." Now Jonah had little time to devote to working on the new home he and Beth would live in. After they were engaged, Jonah had spent another year living in Ohio, fulfilling contracts by carving doors, chairs, mantels, and cabinets for a cabin resort near him. As soon as he'd finished that job, he'd moved here to be near Beth. Since then he'd spent his days carving large items to sell and helping Beth and her aunt Lizzy expand and operate the dry goods store.

Without needing instruction, Jonah steadied the far side

of the closet's doorframe while Gideon leveled and nailed it into place.

They each added the needed hardware and then hung the folding wooden doors. It took a bit of effort to get them on the runners and operating smoothly.

"So what's next, hanging more doors or doing trim work?" Jonah asked.

"Baseboards and window casings. Can't hang doors. There's some sort of holdup on those," Gideon teased. The problem was that Jonah hadn't yet found the time to carve scriptures on them, and Beth didn't want them hung until they were completed. Jonah was capable of carving beautiful scenery, but since this would hang inside his home, he needed to use caution so that no one in the church considered the visual adornments a graven image.

Jonah laughed. "I've assured my fiancée I'll get to them by the time she and I have two or three little ones running around. But regardless of how busy it gets, it feels so good to be living here now. Beth said you moved from here and lived elsewhere for a couple of years, right?"

"Ya." Gideon hoped Jonah wouldn't ask anything else. He did his best not to lie to anyone, but he had secrets to keep. Falsehoods weren't the only thing he detested. He'd hated living in a city away from everything familiar and only returning for the Christmas holidays.

"Jonah." Beth's voice came through the Amish intercom—PVC piping sticking up through the floor and running underground to the store. "Are you at the house?"

Jonah moved closer to the pipe and spoke into it. "Ya. You need something?"

"I'll walk over. I just wanted to be sure you were there."

"We're in the master bedroom."

"Denki."

Gideon chuckled while measuring the length of the wall. "I've always thought Beth had a good head on her shoulders for business."

"She does. She's amazing at it."

Gideon took note of the length of the wall and released the tape measure. "Then how come every time I turn around she's asking you for your opinion? It's like she can't make a decision lately without your input."

Jonah slid an uncut baseboard onto a makeshift bench. "In any serious relationship, if you don't gather your partner's opinion before making a decision that impacts you both, you're just storing up trouble for the future."

Gideon scoffed. "If you figure out a way to avoid trouble in relationships, let me know, okay?"

He measured the board and marked it. Sometimes watching Beth and Jonah interact was like sitting on the porch of an old, run-down trailer while looking at wealthy neighbors. It didn't matter how much he loved them, the reality of their happy relationship chafed.

Three years ago Gideon had let go of the woman he loved. The only woman, really.

He set the wood on the miter box and lowered the battery-powered saw to the board. He never talked to Beth or Jonah about what he had done or why. Actually, he never talked to anyone about it. His family had put together pieces of the truth, but no one discussed it.

Despite Gideon's secretive nature, Jonah seemed to see past his silence. Jonah's perceptiveness was one reason he'd won the heart of the once-wounded and distant Beth Hertzler.

Gideon could only imagine what it'd be like to have the privilege of marrying *the one.* He'd found his *one.* Thoughts of Mattie Lane tormented him. She was…

He stopped his thoughts cold. "Good grief," he mumbled, trying to focus on the work at hand. He took the wood to the base of the wall.

"Having one of those days?" Jonah grabbed one end of the plank, and they set it on the well-placed shims.

"I guess." Gideon hammered nails into his end of the baseboard while Jonah steadied the other end.

Beth's steps echoed through the empty rooms.

Jonah looked up and gave her a welcoming smile that ended quickly. "Something wrong?"

"Remember me telling you about my cousin Mattie, the one I wanted to make our wedding cake?"

Gideon kept pounding in nails as if he had no interest in hearing this conversation. The fact was, he always wanted to know what was happening in Mattie's life. But he could bet money on what Beth was going to say next. Mattie had once again turned down their offer to pay her way home for the wedding and had declined making a cake for their big day.

She didn't return to Apple Ridge often. He knew she had too much business in Berlin, Ohio, to close up shop and come here for a wedding. Even if she could hire someone to fill in for her, she wasn't likely to do so, not even for Beth. He could thank himself for that. Mattie Lane avoided him at all costs. She didn't have to be the one to leave home. He'd left, and he hadn't planned on coming back.

Beth cleared her throat. "Her place burned to the ground this afternoon."

Gideon wheeled around. "What happened?"

"I don't think anyone really knows."

"But Mattie Lane must have some idea how it started."

Beth glanced at Jonah. "She's in the hospital, unconscious."

Dizziness hit Gideon full force, and the hammer in his hand fell to the floor with a thud. *God, not Mattie Lane, please.* "What happened?"

"I can't say for sure. Her sister-in-law called the dry goods store. Aunt Lizzy's taking a message to her parents."

"Beth," Gideon said, "did Dorothy give any indication of how Mattie's doing?"

"She said she has only minor burns, but she inhaled a lot of smoke."

"Smoke inhalation can do as much damage to the insides as flames do to the outside. I don't understand. Her place had excellent smoke detectors."

"How would you know?"

Gideon had made sure Mattie's brother had installed good ones, but he wouldn't tell Beth that. "Go on, Beth."

"Oh, ya." Beth shook her head, as if to refocus her thoughts. "Dorothy said a friend of Mattie's told her that Mattie wasn't at the shop when it caught on fire."

"Then how did she inhale so much smoke?"

"When Mattie arrived, she thought her niece was inside, so she ran into the building, but the shop was empty."

"That's just like her, risking her own life to help when it's not even needed." Gideon wasn't far from having a raging fit.

Beth tilted her head, studying him. "I don't understand you. If you feel this strongly about her, why'd you break up with her to date other girls?"

He rubbed his forehead, trying to control his emotions.

"Even though we aren't together, that doesn't mean I don't care about her well-being. I want what's best for her, and until now that's exactly what she's had. Ya?"

Beth's face creased with lines of concern. "Ya. She loved building up her business and getting better at making decorative cakes." She chuckled. "From the time she was little bitty, she used to get into such fixes, and you always managed to get her out of them." She turned to Jonah. "Mattie is six years younger than me, about three years younger than Gideon. Her ability to create cakes seems boundless, but she can be as flighty as a sparrow."

Beth grinned at Gideon. "Remember when she was fourteen and she won the Hershey's Cocoa Classic contest for her age group? She was so excited that a few minutes after the announcement, she walked straight into a metal pole and about knocked herself unconscious. You grabbed her before she hit the ground and carried her all over those grounds searching for the medic."

Gideon hadn't thought about that in years. "That's classic Mattie Lane." He drew a breath, knowing he had to see her, even at a distance. "Listen, I know you want your home done in time for the wedding to take place here, but I need to check on her for myself. I won't hang around. I just…need to see her."

"We're fine." Jonah picked up the hammer in front of Gideon's feet. "You do what you need to."

Beth pressed a small piece of paper into his hand. "This has the name of the hospital and her room number."

Gideon hurried to the dry goods store and wasted no time calling driver after driver, trying to find someone who could drop what they were doing and take him to see Mattie Lane, hopefully one who didn't mind pushing the speed limit a little.

Sol went ahead of the other three hunters, going deeper and deeper into the woods. He could hear them talking as they trailed behind.

He took a deep whiff of the air around him. Cold and earthy. He loved the outdoors. The restlessness of the nocturnal creatures after the sun began to slip behind the horizon. The brilliance of stars at this time of year. The beauty of being in a tree stand as dark yielded to the first rays of the sun. The exuberance of the animals at daybreak.

He wished Mattie would come with him just once. They didn't have to hunt. A perfect spot on a hill or in a tree stand and a pair of binoculars was all she'd need to learn that everything worth doing in a day didn't take place inside her cake shop.

He spotted the clearing of the campsite some twenty feet

ahead. As soon as he arrived at the camp, he quickly set up his tent, and while the others put up theirs, he gathered wood and started a fire. The campsite had level ground, a fire pit, and a creek that provided both fresh water and the gurgling sound he loved to hear while falling asleep.

Within an hour they'd had a simple meal of hot dogs and were sitting around the fire ready to talk about nothing.

"Hey, Sol." Amish Henry sat on a nearby rock with his forearms propped on his knees. "The three of us have been wondering about something."

"Ya, what's that?"

"You couldn't get a girl before Mattie, and now that you have her, others are looking your way. It's like you had to get a girl to catch the eye of a girl."

Nothing felt as right as having Mattie. He had someone to think about wherever he was and someone to go home to.

"You know, what Amish Henry said is true," Daniel added.

Sol hadn't really thought about it but had noticed a few girls looking his way during singings and at church services. "I've never asked to take a girl home from a singing. Not even Mattie."

"Plenty of older single guys were ready to fight over her," Daniel said. "What'd you do different?"

"Nothing. When she came up to me after the singings, I

talked to her. She didn't mind that I didn't have much to say. I wanted to ask to take her home, but I couldn't. Not then. I think I could now. Maybe it's not having a girl to get a girl as much as having confidence."

"Ya," Daniel said. "You're confident you're not interested in anyone else, and suddenly other girls are looking your way."

"Wait," Amish Henry said. "You mean *she* asked *you*?"

"Hey," Sol said, trying to change the subject, "Mattie packed five cupcakes." As Sol rose to his feet, he noticed shafts of light splashing here and there. "I think I see flashlights coming toward us." Sol strode that way. "Hello?"

"We're looking for Sol Bender."

A beam of light flashed in his face. "You found me."

"We've been looking for you since four o'clock. Mattie's brother sent us…"

Their voices muffled in his ears. The night air closed in around him, and everything that had seemed right about coming here became heavy.

❧

After forty-five minutes of calling every driver he knew, Gideon found one. Twenty minutes later Gary arrived at the dry goods store, and they began the trek to the hospital in Berlin. Gary flipped radio stations and tried to engage Gideon in conversation the whole way, but it was the longest, most miserable six-hour trip he'd ever made.

Thoughts of Mattie Lane tormented him. He didn't care how cliché it sounded—there was not another woman like her.

She had a smile that all but swallowed her. When she was tickled about something, which happened often, her cheeks turned a color similar to her reddish-blond hair. It wasn't a blush as much as her enthusiasm glowing from within.

She had a gentle side and would do anything for those she loved. Even as a little girl and teen, when she was given the slightest chance to get free of the heaviness and concerns over her mother's chronic illness, Mattie Lane radiated joy—like sunlight streaming through storm clouds.

But when her mother had become seriously ill six years ago, Mattie Lane struggled. She'd deny it, but he knew the truth, had witnessed it time and again—the tragedies of others weighed more on her than on most folks. And he imagined that the destruction of her property would be crushing.

Gary yawned as he entered the hospital's parking lot. It'd been dark for most of the trip here, but the clock on the dashboard said it was only eleven. He stopped the car near the front of the hospital. "I'll park and then go to the waiting room on her floor."

"Thanks." Gideon jumped out and hurried through the automatic doors. He barely took note of anything as he rode the elevator to the third floor. He walked past the nurses' station, found Mattie Lane's room, and opened the door.

His chest physically hurt when he saw her. She didn't look like herself at all. Her face was pale, and she wore no prayer Kapp. A large patch of gauze was taped to the side of her neck, and it continued down past the edge of her hospital gown. A small white tube hung from the side of her mouth, and a larger beige one was attached to her arm. A plastic apparatus on her right index finger glowed.

"Hello," said a female voice, and he looked up. The woman, wearing a blue uniform, stood at the head of Mattie Lane's bed, messing with a bag of liquid. She smiled. "Visiting hours are over. I sent the rest of her family home awhile ago."

"I came as soon as I heard, and it took me hours to get here."

"Ah, then I suppose you can stay for a little bit."

"Is…she okay?"

"She will be."

"Are you sure?"

"Yes," she said quietly. "Dr. Grady said she's a lucky young woman. Emotionally traumatized, but she sustained relatively few physical injuries."

Relief hit so hard it made his legs weak. A machine behind her head indicated that her heart rate was strong and steady. And other than the gauze traipsing down the right side of her neck and shoulder, she didn't have many outward signs of wounds. But fresh fears began to surface.

"Any internal injuries?"

"I can't give out that kind of information, but I can say that she's had every necessary test run and is receiving the proper treatment."

"Has she woken up?"

"Yes, for a few minutes here and there, but she's groggy from being put to sleep for some of the tests. I imagine she'll be released in a day or two."

Gideon sank into a chair, whispering thanks to God as the woman left. He missed Mattie so much it hurt, but he'd done the right thing. He knew he had.

Her face reflected pain as she shifted. Her eyes opened for a brief second, then closed again. "You're here," she whispered hoarsely.

"I'm here, Mattie Lane."

A faint smile crossed her lips, and she reached for him. His heart thudded wildly, latching on to these few moments. Desire for a life with her swept him away, and needlelike pinpricks ran over his skin from his head to his feet.

Just a few more moments with her—surely God would grant him that much.

He took her limp hand in his and was rendered powerless by the connection. It'd been so long since he'd felt the soft, delicate skin of her fingers. Confusion enclosed his thoughts. What was he doing? He'd broken up with her for good reasons, ones that stood almost as insurmountable today as they were then.

Almost.

She squeezed his hand. His mind went crazy with longing. But a clear vision of what little he had to offer her splashed icy water on his hopes.

"S...s..." Her eyes fluttered but didn't open.

His mouth went dry. She wanted Sol Bender. Of course she did, and that's how it should be. Maybe her feathery light smile moments ago hadn't been because she'd seen or heard him. Who knew what she was aware of or thinking as she drifted in and out of consciousness? No matter who she called for, Gideon had to get out before she opened her eyes and saw him. Easing her hand onto the bed, he stood.

"Gideon?" she whispered.

Finding it hard to breathe, he turned to leave. A man wearing camouflage gear stood in the doorway. He swallowed hard. Gideon had opened the door for Sol to walk into Mattie's life, yet jealousy clawed at him.

Had Sol heard Mattie whisper his name?

Gideon shifted. "The reports were vague, so I came to check on her."

Faint recognition of some sort went through Sol's eyes. "Have we met?"

He forced himself to hold out his hand—this man was Mattie's future, after all. "Gideon Beiler."

The expression on Sol's face showed disbelief. "You're kidding me."

Embarrassment smothered Gideon. How could he possibly justify being here?

"Sol Bender." He finally shook his hand. "She and I are together now, have been for a while."

Gideon swallowed hard. He racked his brain, trying to think of the right thing to say. "I know it may not seem like it, but I'm glad for her."

Skepticism entered Sol's eyes before he went to the far side of the bed and touched the back of her hand. "Mattie?"

She didn't respond. But her smooth face and rhythmic breathing indicated she was sleeping peacefully...obviously soothed by her boyfriend's presence.

"Mattie?" Sol repeated as he cradled her hand, but she didn't rouse.

Gideon felt like an intruder, but he couldn't make himself leave.

Sol peeled out of his hunting jacket. "You can stay if you want to," he mumbled. "But she's not going to like that you're here. It'll just add more stress." Sol gently brushed hair off her forehead.

Gideon steadied the ache inside his chest. He'd done the right thing to end their relationship. He was sure of it, and if given a chance to do that time over, he'd set her free again. But that didn't make seeing her in love with someone else any easier.

Four

Mattie stood in front of her brother's home, her mood as dark and cold as the night surrounding her. The street lamps peered through the fog as Sol loaded her bags into the rig. She'd shared Thanksgiving earlier today at her brother's place. Dorothy had made quite a feast, but Mattie had barely stomached eating. All she could see in her mind's eye was the ruins of Mattie Cakes.

Her brother put a fresh car battery in the floorboard and attached wires to it so the headlights worked. "I know you don't want to go back to Pennsylvania right now, but there's nothing you can do here until we get the issues settled with the insurance company, and that's going to take about four weeks. Then we can look for a place to rent and convert it into a usable bakeshop until we can rebuild this spring." James put his hand on her shoulder. "Besides, Mamm wants her only daughter to come home for a while after all that's happened. And I think maybe you could use a little time away from here."

She gazed at where Mattie Cakes had stood only a week earlier. Through the foggy night air, she could see the jagged, charred remnants of her shop two hundred feet away. She was grateful the flames and sparks hadn't set any other buildings on fire. But the old wood Mattie Cakes was built with had ignited like a box of kitchen matches, and her ovens, pans, utensils, and supplies had melted or been damaged beyond repair. The worst loss was her scrapbook with all her notes, pictures, and magazine cutouts of specialty cakes.

Dorothy hugged her. "As soon as we get the insurance straightened out, we'll buy the materials to rebuild. Then in the spring we'll have a shop raising to rival any barn raising you've ever witnessed."

"Denki." Mattie held her tight, not wanting to leave the place she now called home. But she released her and climbed into the rig.

Her parents had made the trip here last week, visiting her in the hospital every day until she was released. Then Mamm had returned to Pennsylvania a couple of days ago, needing to get ready for the traditional Thanksgiving meal at her home with her six other sons and their wives and children. But once Mamm got home, she couldn't rest with Mattie elsewhere, so she beckoned her daughter to return to Apple Ridge. Mattie's siblings were concerned about Mamm and were also urging

Mattie to come—without any further delay for Mamm's sake. So here she was, at the end of Thanksgiving Day, miserable, and yet packed and headed to Pennsylvania.

No one expected to be able to rebuild the shop in the dead of winter, but she wasn't staying in Pennsylvania until warmer weather arrived. She'd managed to talk Mamm into letting her return to Ohio in time for Christmas so she and Sol could attend the Christmas singing together.

Sol climbed in beside her. He took the reins in hand and slapped them against the horse's back as she waved to James and Dorothy. The clip-clop of the hoofs against the pavement echoed in the quietness, and she settled back in her seat. Sol eased his hand over hers as he drove toward Strasburg, where they'd meet up with a driver who'd agreed to take her to the train station. Later, a woman named Gloria, who often drove her cousin Beth, would meet Mattie at the station in Pennsylvania.

Mattie tried to steady her pounding heart by reminding herself that the journey ahead was simply keeping the promise she'd made to come home if Mamm ever needed her. But the rampant thudding inside her chest reminded her that giving one's word was much easier than keeping it.

As soon as she arrived in Pennsylvania, she needed to finish contacting all her clients to cancel their orders. All her records had been lost in the fire, but she'd called every person she could remember in order to cancel orders that had been made. Her thoughts were too cloudy to recall everyone. It'd be awful if someone showed up at her store expecting a cake and saw the shop in ashes.

If she could find a place in Berlin to keep working, she would. But baking decorative cakes required ample workspace and a large oven. Dorothy's kitchen couldn't accommodate Mattie's needs, nor could Mackenzie's shop. Mattie didn't want to cancel all the orders for the next four to six months, but she could think of no solutions, and she was heartsick over it.

The midnight jaunt to Strasburg left Mattie feeling as if she were a character in one of those old movies playing in the Englischer homes where she used to baby-sit. Danger always lurked in the misty darkness.

Even under the shroud of night, Sol looked capable and relaxed. She wished she could be more like him in that way. "As skittish as a horse on a highway" defined her personality of late, but changes in plans, even unfair ones, never shook Sol.

He glanced her way and smiled.

"Would you sing for me?"

He put his arm around her shoulders, and she moved in closer while he sang, *"Welcher nun Gott mill lieben thun."* As he sang, she considered the lyrics—"Whoever now wants to love God, let him first love his brother. Lay down his life for him, as Christ gave Himself for us in death…out of love and mercy."

Was Sol trying to tell her that she needed to be more gracious about having to go home? Irritability churned inside her as it had ever since she woke up in the hospital. She had to constantly fight the urge to gripe or cry about everything.

He pulled in front of the driver's home, brought the rig to a halt, and turned off the lights. "You'll be back before you know it."

The front door of the home opened, and Sharon Wells held up one finger. "Be there in just a few." She disappeared into her home again.

Sharon had driven Mattie to and from the train station whenever Mattie needed a lift. It was too far to drive a rig to the station in Alliance, and not many drivers were willing to take her there at one in the morning.

Another round of sadness swept through Mattie. She longed for the comfort of her shop, its vanilla scent and the warmth of the oven. "Could you please think of something soothing to say?"

Sol removed his hat and scratched his head. "Your folks asked, and you agreed." He got out of the rig, went around to her side of the buggy, and opened the door. "They've paid for two drivers and a train ticket. You can't get cold feet now."

That didn't make her feel any better, but she knew that he intended for his no-nonsense explanation to be comforting. She climbed out as he grabbed her bags. "You didn't pack much."

"I'd have even less if Mackenzie hadn't given me a stack of magazines to take with me. Most of my belongings were in the attic room of my shop. I've already told you that."

"Yep, you did. I was just making sure you hadn't left something behind." He set the luggage down.

She chuckled. "You are such a liar, Sol Bender. You know good and well that you simply forgot I'd told you."

He swallowed her in a gentle hug. "Who is going to keep me straight while you're gone?"

She waited for the strength of his arms to absorb some of her nervousness. "No one if you know what's good for you."

He tilted her chin upward. "No matter how long you're gone, I'll be as faithful as if you were standing next to me."

Sol wasn't much of a talker. He usually said what he needed to express in quips or shy smiles. But he understood what she needed from him. She wiped fresh tears off her cheeks. "I'm so sick of crying."

"Well, we agree on that at least." He was teasing her, but she was sure her recent behavior had taxed him. "Maybe you need this trip, Mattie."

"Oh, you just want to get rid of me so you can return to your hunting free of all guilt."

He kissed her. "Can't blame a guy for trying."

She backed away and pulled an envelope from her purse. "This is the number to Hertzlers' store. It'll be the easiest way to get a message to me." She'd given him this information twice already, but if she knew Sol, he'd already misplaced it. He was a lot like her when it came to misplacing things. But on nights like this, when she needed his help at one in the morning, he never muttered the slightest complaint.

Sharon came out of her home and unlocked her van.

Sol put her luggage in the trunk and closed it. He stifled a yawn as he waited for Mattie to get in the passenger's seat. She waved, and he held up four fingers, representing the weeks she'd be gone.

Her frustration surfaced again. Mattie Cakes stayed so busy during the holidays, and she loved every minute of it. She'd miss all the hustle and bustle of getting brightly decorated cakes out the door to become a part of people's feasts and celebrations.

She'd thought that coming to Ohio three years ago was God giving her beauty for ashes—the shop and Sol. But now Mattie Cakes was nothing but ashes, and Sol's favorite thing about her—her ability to remain on an even keel emotionally—had also gone up in smoke. Had she displeased God somehow and this was His way of getting her attention?

At least one good thing would come from this change of plans. She'd be able to make the cakes for her aunt Lizzy's and her cousin Beth's weddings. Lizzy was actually Mattie's step-aunt. Lizzy and her siblings came from the second marriage of Mattie's grandfather. As a widower, he'd married a younger woman, so now the siblings and stepsiblings ranged in age from Rebecca at seventy to Lizzy at forty.

Even though Lizzy was forty, she never had a beau until she and the widower bishop fell in love. It was an odd coincidence that Beth and Lizzy, who'd run Hertzlers' Dry Goods together for years, were getting married less than two weeks apart.

Beth was more than a decade younger than Lizzy and had buried her first fiancé. Mattie had never seen anyone take the death of a loved one harder than Beth had. But two years ago Beth had met Jonah Kinsinger, and shortly after, it was revealed why she had shut herself off from everyone after Henry died. He hadn't been who he pretended to be, and when Beth realized it, she ended their engagement. Whether by accident or on purpose, later that night he drowned in a river.

Henry and Gideon had more in common than Mattie wanted to admit. Both men hid parts of who they were from everyone. Gideon wasn't abusive like Henry, but she was floored by his interest in non-Amish women.

She watched the lights in the distance as the driver headed for the train station. Regardless of her sadness over losing her business, she was looking forward to meeting the new man in Beth's life. Somehow Jonah Kinsinger had brought truth and healing to Beth, and Mattie intended to hug him for it.

As the lights of various towns came and went, she wondered what had changed Gideon. She'd known him his whole life. Beth had been caught by surprise at who Henry really was, but he hadn't grown up around them. Gideon's grandmother's farmhouse sat across the street from her parents' place. When they were little and he stayed the night with his grandmother, they waved at each other from their bedrooms and talked on the two-way radios until one of them fell asleep. As teens they used sign language…and the two-way radio. Once they'd even sent messages back and forth tied to the mane of a horse. Because he lived with his parents in a different district some twenty miles away, they didn't attend the same Amish school or the same church, but she'd been certain she knew the real Gideon.

She used to think that marrying him would mean spending the rest of her life with her best friend. As it turned out, he wasn't a friend at all—not to her and probably not to himself either.

It wouldn't affect her one way or the other, but she couldn't help wondering if he'd changed any in the last three years.

Five

With a fresh supply of screws in hand, Gideon left the dry goods store. Cold air seeped across the land as if someone had opened a huge freezer. While he strode across the parking lot, he studied the outside of Beth and Jonah's unfinished home, mentally calculating what he needed to finish.

After several holdups due to supplies and weather, he couldn't afford another setback. Workwise he had lost only half a day when Mattie was hurt. But emotionally he'd yet to regain his footing. Something hard inside him had dislodged when he feared for her safety, and he needed to get it back in place. Since he hadn't told her the truth about why he broke up with her, she might always hold a grudge.

Determined to accept his fate, he tried to focus on the job in front of him—finishing Beth and Jonah's place. The couple could have their wedding at her parents' place and live in Beth's apartment above Hertzlers' Dry Goods until the house was completed. But Gideon had given his word he'd finish it on time.

Car tires crunched against gravel in the store's parking lot. Gideon glanced behind him, and his heart threatened to stop.

Mattie Lane sat in the car with Beth's driver for the store. Jonah had mentioned that Gloria brought Mattie home from the bus station early this morning.

Relief at seeing her strong enough to be out once again washed over him. But he still would rather not face her. Had Sol told her about his visit to the hospital?

Trying to avoid looking Mattie's way, Gideon went up the wooden steps and into the house. A layer of chalky dust covered the walls, ceilings, and particle board floors. Kitchen cabinets stood in the center of the room, waiting for him to secure them to the newly finished walls. Leftover wood trim was stacked along one wall. Tubs, sinks, and commodes were still in their boxes, sitting in odd places, along with various types of hardware. But right now he intended to hang a few doors.

The cold and empty disarray of the place made him feel as if he'd stepped inside his own soul. In all his planning and calculations to set Mattie free, he hadn't anticipated what his life would be like if he survived the cancer. He'd spent the better part of two years in a hospital, much of it quarantined. Not one doctor had expected him to beat the blast crisis phase. The journey from the day he was diagnosed to today had changed him so much he no longer recognized himself.

Ignoring the weight of that thought, he kept his outward movements as normal as any other day, hoping to convince anyone who might see him—like someone from Beiler Construction stopping by or the visitors Beth, Jonah, and Lizzy regularly gave tours to—that he was fine. But he couldn't fool himself. His dry mouth and clammy palms spoke truth. His mind hadn't let him sleep the last few nights, and his heart couldn't decide whether to race or to stop beating altogether.

The destruction he'd faced since learning he had chronic myelogenous leukemia seemed infinite. When he was first diagnosed, he was in early chronic phase, and his survival rate was ninety percent, so he quietly traveled to Philadelphia for treatment, thinking he could keep it from Mattie until he had a clean bill of health. But while in treatment, his abnormal white cells had exploded in growth, and with it his chance of survival plummeted. So did he, but he'd shored himself up as best he could, while keeping his diagnosis from everyone in Apple Ridge. The battle with cancer had stolen nearly every piece of who he was. If anyone could destroy what little he had left, Mattie Lane could. She hated him for cheating on her.

Regardless of how she felt, he had to find a way to peacefully deal with her over the weeks ahead.

After moving two freshly carved doors from the back porch to the appropriate spots to hang them, he put on his tool belt and went into the master bathroom. Gideon attached a set of hinges to the frame of the doorway, then used his foot as a prop to help balance the door while tapping the pin into the hinge with a hammer.

"Gideon," Jonah called as he entered the home.

"Master bathroom."

When Jonah came to the room, Gideon opened the door he was trying to hang just enough to let Jonah enter.

With a cane in one hand, Jonah held out his other hand for the hammer. Gideon gave it to him, glad for the help. He dug into his tool belt and pulled two more hinge pins.

Jonah took them and tapped one into place. "I think you should get the kitchen cabinets in place next."

"But you haven't finished carving on them."

"There's been a change of plans. We'll put them up as is."

"Okay, but why?"

The sound of female voices caused Gideon to shift his attention to the window.

Mattie Lane and Beth were heading this way. Mattie was dressed like an Ohio Amish woman now, with the stiffer oval prayer Kapp and a sage green apron that matched her dress. Like him, she'd joined the Old Order Amish faith about two years ago. It was below forty with the wind blowing, and she wasn't wearing a coat.

Her eyes grew large with pleasure as she studied the new home, and a part of him he'd buried long ago rattled against its confinement. She pointed out various details and smiled as she hugged Beth.

Mattie Lane. Energetic. Vibrant. Talented. Poised. And beautiful inside and out. She was also scattered, easily distracted, and had a jealous streak the size of Pennsylvania. When it came to ending their relationship with a lie, he used her jealousy against her to set her free from his doomed future.

Jonah's cane thudded against the particle board as he moved closer to the window. "Look at them, Gideon."

"I did." The familiar hardness took control again, and he turned back to his work. "I saw two half-giddy women gabbing ninety to nothing."

"Ya, sharing encouragement and excitement. Menfolk would never do that…except maybe with a girlfriend or wife."

"The day a man needs that kind of nonsense is the day he might as well accept that he's not really a man at all."

Jonah laughed. "Not a man, eh?"

The sound of the front door swooshing open started a war inside Gideon.

If she knew he had come to the hospital to see her, he could discount his rash action by saying he'd overreacted to hearing that she'd been hurt. But his nervous shaking reminded him that he had deeper secrets to keep and a heart to guard.

Hers.

Gideon motioned toward the bedroom door. "I'd like to get that door up next." *And close it.*

Gideon grabbed the door and laid it on the sawhorses so he could get the hardware on it.

"Jonah?" Beth called.

He stepped toward the doorway, and the women entered.

Beth looped her arm through her fiancé's. "And this is Jonah."

Mattie Lane's hands were tucked inside her folded arms, probably in an effort to stay warm, but her smile embraced Jonah. "I think she might be just a tad in love with you."

Gideon tried to pull his attention back to the job at hand—mounting hardware on the door.

"A tad is not nearly a success," Jonah said. "Mattie Lane, right?"

The use of her pet name caused Gideon to cringe, and he looked up.

The smile on her face faded. "Why would you call me that?"

Jonah glanced at Gideon, and Mattie noticed him for the

first time since entering the room. Her pale blue eyes stayed glued to him, as if she were too shocked to move. Gideon hadn't realized he'd used that name when talking to Jonah, but he'd called her by that nickname since she was twelve, telling her that a day with her was a journey all by itself—a trip down a one-of-a-kind country road, Mattie Lane.

Finally she nodded. "Gideon."

"Hi." All the months of aching for her that had painstakingly turned into years rushed from their buried place and leveled him.

She looked back at Jonah. "It's just Mattie." She held out her hand and shook Jonah's. "I'm so glad to finally meet you. Beth's told me a lot about you in her letters." She entered the room and peeked into the full bathroom. "I'm completely awed by this home. You've done an amazing job."

Jonah shoved his hammer into his tool belt. "Gideon's been doing everything from the contracting to the finishing carpentry while I've spent the better part of this past year helping Beth and Lizzy expand the product line for the dry goods store."

Mattie glanced at Gideon as though he were some half-remembered acquaintance from her past. She shifted her attention out the window. "You have a perfect view of the store."

"And look." Beth took Mattie to the PVC piping that was

the conduit for the Amish intercom. "It's a direct line from the store to here. The workers can easily contact us this way."

Mattie chuckled. "I could've used one of these between Mattie Cakes and my brother's place."

"The intercom system was Gideon's idea," Beth said. "He dug the trench to lay the pipe and installed it for us."

An unfamiliar look entered Mattie's eyes, as if anything to do with him disgusted her. She moved to the bathroom door. In bold scroll Jonah had carved "Charity endureth all things."

"What a beautiful carving." She rubbed her arms.

"Ya. Jonah's work is what drew me to him," Beth said. "I saw a scene carved on a small stump in a store in Ohio and wanted to purchase more just like it for our store."

Gideon took off his coat and held it out to Mattie. "The heat will be in working order next week."

She shook her head. "Denki. But I'm fine."

"Oh," Beth exclaimed. "I was so excited to show you around, I didn't even notice you were freezing."

"I took off my coat in Gloria's car. She had it really hot in there while we were running errands in town for Mamm, and I forgot to grab it before she drove off."

Beth frowned. "Seems like you would've thought about it the moment you got out of the car."

Mattie shrugged. "One would think…"

Gideon knew that when Mattie had one thing on her mind, like seeing Beth, she didn't notice much else until she was in a fix and needed rescuing.

Gideon thrust the coat toward her. "Take it, Mattie Lane."

Her eyes flashed with an anger much deeper than anything to do with her refusal to borrow his coat. "Do not snap orders at me, Gideon." She spoke each word slowly, issuing both a boundary line of how to treat her and a threat of a volcanic-sized eruption.

Gideon couldn't help but chuckle. She'd outgrown being overly nice to everyone, and he was glad to see it. "Finally standing up for yourself. Good for you."

She moved toward the doorway. "Beth, I'd like to see the rest of your house. And Jonah's new workshop."

When he realized his comment had come off as an insult, he flinched. Beth's brow creased with concern before she placed her arm protectively around Mattie's shoulders. "Sure."

Jonah motioned for the women to go on without him.

Gideon stepped ahead of them. "I'm sorry. That was rude. I can't believe I blurted that out."

After staring ahead for several long moments, Mattie turned to Beth. "Can I have a minute with Gideon?"

"Ya. Sure." Beth took Jonah's hand, and they went down the hallway.

Now that they were alone and could speak freely, Gideon would soon know whether Sol had told her about his visit to the hospital.

She studied Gideon. "I've always had a backbone. Any confusion I had about when to use it was your fault, not mine."

He wasn't sure exactly what in their past made that statement true, but he nodded. "I ask your forgiveness for thinking otherwise."

The Amish ways forced her to forgive him, so he felt no sense of release when she said, "Forgiven."

He held out the coat. "In that case…"

Her eyes, sizing him up, carried disrespect. He still didn't know if Sol had told her about his visit. She wasn't as easy to read as he'd expected.

She took the coat from him and slipped it on and, after buttoning it, waggled her shoulders as if enjoying its warmth. "Anything that keeps you uncomfortable while doing the opposite for me works for me. Thanks."

She shoved her hands into the pockets and left.

Gideon sighed. He had set her free, and she'd prospered from it. She'd gone to Ohio and built a successful business and met Sol. He'd expected her coolness toward him, but he was beginning to question if he could ever be content with it.

Six

Mattie got up from the dinner table and began stacking plates. Oddly enough, after barely stomaching the Thanksgiving meal yesterday with her brother and his family, she'd enjoyed having leftovers today with her parents.

Her mom stood.

"Mamm, take your cue from Daed, and sit." Mattie patted her mother's thin, delicate skin.

Daed's gray hair had the shape of having worn a hat all day. "Ya, Rebecca. What other child do you have who'll wash dishes?"

Mattie laughed. "The price one pays for having so many sons."

Mamm sat back down at the table, her eyes bright in spite of the new wrinkles weighing on her eyelids. Mattie's brothers had been right. She'd needed to come home and spend extra time with their mother.

"Verna came by today while you were out," Mamm said.

"She was bent on seeing you. I promised her you'd walk over there tonight."

Mattie put the dishes in the sink, wishing her mother hadn't told Gideon's grandmother she'd visit. She'd seen Gideon ride bareback past the front window a few minutes ago. While he was working on Beth and Jonah's home, he was probably staying with his grandmother rather than trekking back and forth from his parents' place.

His winter jacket hung on the coatrack in the front hallway, and he could go the whole winter without it for all she cared.

"Mattie?" Mamm called.

She turned. "I don't want to go tonight. Can it wait until tomorrow?"

"I suppose. But I gave my word, and you're obviously feeling well enough to walk across the street."

Daed shifted his chair away from the table. "I agree with your Mamm. I don't want us to have to make up an excuse for why you're not up to seeing her."

Mattie stared at Gideon's coat, hating the idea of having to be nice to him.

Mamm followed her gaze. "What's wrong?"

Unwilling to burden her mom with petty emotions that should have been long dead by now, she kissed her cheek. "Not a thing. I'll go see Verna."

"She'll be so pleased."

She put on the coat Gloria had dropped by the house a few hours ago, then grabbed Gideon's. Crossing the narrow street, she coached herself on how to speak gently. She climbed the two stone steps, knocked on the door, and waited.

Verna opened the door. "Mattie." She hugged her warmly. *"Kumm mol rei."*

Mattie stepped inside, warmth and the smell of dinner surrounding her. "It's good to see you. How are you?"

"Fair to middling for a woman my age. I sure was sorry to hear about your cake shop. I remember a couple of years ago when Gideon told your brother about—"

"Mammi Beiler," Gideon interrupted. He stood at the kitchen table with a plate of pancakes and bacon. "Kumm eat." He set it on the table.

"Oh, he fixed a meal for me. I'm having breakfast for dinner because yesterday I sent all the Thanksgiving food home with his Mamm. I should go see if it's any good before it gets cold." Verna went to a chair and sat.

Gideon walked to Mattie and held out his hand for the coat. "Thanks."

He didn't look like the man she'd once loved. That man had been carefree and gentle. This one seemed hardened and weary. Maybe trying to keep an Amish girlfriend while dating Englischer girls did that to a man.

She gave it to him. "Denki for the use of it."

"Not a problem."

"It's clearly mealtime, and I should go." She turned to Verna. "Good to see you. Maybe you can slip over one morning before I go home. We could have hot chocolate in front of the roaring fire like we used to."

"And maybe some oddly shaped coffeecake?" Verna asked.

Mattie laughed. "Sure. But if they come out oddly shaped these days, it'll be intentional on my part."

"That reminds me." She stood. "I have something for you. Wait right here." She headed for the stairs. "Make yourself comfortable. I'm going to be a few minutes."

Gideon moved to the stove. "Care for some hot tea?"

"No." The word came out harsher than she'd intended. It wouldn't have been easy to be nice to him under the best of circumstances, and she was far from her best self.

He stole a sideways glance before grabbing the kettle off the stove. He reached into a cabinet and pulled down the delicate china cup she'd always used when visiting here. He rinsed and dried it. "I know it's been rough for you lately." He set a variety of tea bags on the table and poured hot water into her cup.

She dumped the cup of steaming water into the sink. "Please don't act like you're my friend."

The muscles in his jaw tightened. "I didn't mean to offend you."

That was the problem. Everything about him offended her. "How's Ashley?"

Surprise reflected in his eyes for a moment. "I haven't seen her in a while."

"Ya." She wrinkled her nose. "It's hard to keep the decent ones around when you keep cheating on them."

Hardness entered his eyes. "Give it a rest, Mattie Lane."

She took a seat across the table from him, wishing she was in Ohio baking and decorating cakes. And wishing he'd stop calling her Mattie Lane.

They both stared at the kitchen table, and she wondered if he was thinking about the same thing she was—the day she caught him with Ashley.

It'd been Christmas Day. They'd attended the annual Christmas singing on her birthday the night before. She'd enjoyed it as much as ever, except Gideon hadn't been his usual fun-loving self. When he hugged her good night, he said he was really tired and wouldn't come over on Christmas. Actually, he'd been using exhaustion as an excuse for weeks, and he'd said the doctor thought he might have mono. So she'd wanted to do something special to help him feel loved until he was on his feet again.

She spent all day making a beautiful Christmas cake to take to him, and she wrote a love letter as part of her Christmas present. She hired a driver to take her the twenty miles to his parents' home in Plainview.

With his gifts in tow, she arrived at his parents' place. Gideon lived in a tiny house less than a stone's throw from his parents, but as a single woman, she couldn't visit him there.

When his mother opened the door, she stammered something about Gideon not being around and reluctantly invited her in. Mattie tried to have their usual relaxed conversation, but Susie was obviously upset.

Mattie wondered what was going on. If Gideon didn't feel well enough to come to her place on Christmas Day, why wasn't he at home resting? She visited for a minute before leaving the cake.

She hadn't been willing to leave her love letter with his parents, so she went to his little home across the yard, intending to shove it under the door. When she reached his doorstep, she heard voices. She started to knock on the window of the door but then caught a glimpse of him through the curtains. He was holding a woman with long, free-flowing black hair, dressed in jeans and a silky gold jacket. An Englischer.

Jealousy flew over her. Nothing was as insulting as a Plain man wanting a fancy woman. Mattie followed the ways of their people, and he was supposed to respect and honor that, not go chasing after something…someone different.

She opened the door. Gideon and the girl jumped, looking as guilty as forbidden lovers caught in the act. "What's going on?"

"Mattie." Gideon was breathless. "What are you doing here?"

"Answer my question. What is going on?" She said each word deliberately.

The woman began to cry. "Tell her, Gideon."

He rubbed his forehead, a habit he had when trying to figure out what to do. "Okay, Ashley, I will."

The girl's eyes widened. "You're finally going to tell her the truth?"

Finally? How long had Gideon been seeing this Englischer woman?

"Go on home and rest. I'll be over later tonight." He escorted Ashley to the door.

Once she was gone, he turned to Mattie. "I…I'd hoped we could get through the holidays before…"

Mattie's head spun, and her body felt as if it had turned to lead. "Tell me now, Gideon. Right now."

"I…I think it's best if you see other people. You've never dated anyone else. And I need to be free too."

Mattie shook all over, trying her best not to cry. "What? Why?"

"It's the way it needs to be." His voice wavered, and he cleared his throat. "I'm sorry."

He had feelings for her. She could see that even as he broke up with her. But they weren't enough for him. She'd seen him with Englischer girls before. She'd only been fifteen the first time she saw him getting out of a girl's car. But he always had some excuse—she'd had a flat tire, and he'd helped change it before she gave him a lift, or she was a stranger dropping by his house to see if he wanted a free puppy.

The night she saw him with Ashley, she had no choice but to set him free and go live with her brother as quickly as she could pack up all her baking equipment.

For three years she'd put her heart and soul into building a new life. And she'd done everything in her power to avoid thinking about Gideon. But seeing him now, in the flesh, brought back memories of all she'd held dear. She'd loved him. But what can be done when the one you love doesn't feel the same way?

Mattie looked up from the kitchen table, wishing she'd accepted that cup of tea after all. "I've met someone."

Gideon's jaw clenched. "I'm happy for you." He brushed his hand along the edge of the table. "That being the case, can we let go of the past and get along as friends?"

"I'll try." She played with her empty cup. "I will."

Verna came into the kitchen with a stack of used cake pans. "I've been collecting these for years. Didn't know why, 'cause you had plenty of your own. But now maybe they'll help." She set them on the table in front of Mattie.

"Oh, Verna, this is so kind of you." Mattie lifted each one. There were heart-shaped, round, rectangular, Bundt, square, and ring pans. "Denki."

Tears clouded her vision. The pain of losing her shop and everything in it still rattled her very soul.

Gideon stared into his mug, looking uncomfortable. "I know you'll consider that what I'm about to say are the words of a man who thinks everything and everyone can be replaced. But you'll rebuild. Whatever the insurance company doesn't cover, the communities—both here and there—will."

She should simply nod, but the need to tell someone who would understand pressed in hard. "I lost the notebook."

It seemed that grief and disappointment ran through his eyes, and she found a measure of comfort in his compassion for her loss.

After he'd given her the notebook, they'd spent years going places to get ideas for creating cakes and had filled the book with rough sketches they'd drawn and pictures they'd cut out of cake-decorating magazines. She could feel his laughter wash over her as they went through museums, trying to draw ideas as they came up with them when neither one of them was any good at freehand art.

He used to take her to Front Street in Harrisburg, and they would stroll along the Susquehanna. Watching the river was what gave her the idea for her rough-ride icing, which was a huge hit with customers. Then the two of them would eat at the Fire House Restaurant, a renovated fire station built in the eighteen hundreds. Between Gideon's ideas and other sites in Harrisburg, she'd garnered a lot of her cake-making ideas.

As she sat across from him, remembering so many of their dates, she realized how self-absorbed she'd been. Did they ever do something he enjoyed?

She looked up and met his green eyes, wanting to acknowledge that maybe she had played more of a part in their breakup than she'd admitted. But she couldn't say it, not without asking why he hadn't talked to her about what bothered him in their relationship *before* he cheated.

"I guess the notebook was a little like us—years in the making and destroyed in just a few minutes." Mattie gathered her pans. "Well, I'm just a bright spot right now, aren't I? I think I'll take my gloom elsewhere for a bit."

Verna hugged her. "You'll feel better in a few weeks, and you'll get back on your feet again in a matter of months. You always do."

Between her mother's health issues and Gideon's betrayal, she'd faced her share of difficult times in life. "You're right. I always do."

Seven

*W*ind pushed against the enclosed buggy, making it rock unsteadily, as Gideon drove toward Zook's Diner under the dark morning sky. He pulled onto the gravel parking lot, hopped out, and looped the strap around a hitching post.

The aroma of breakfast foods filled the air even before he opened the glass door. He walked through the tiny convenience store attached to the diner and headed straight to the pass-through that separated the restaurant from the kitchen. The place had the typical look of an outdated diner: cement floors, well-worn Formica tabletops, and a long counter with accompanying swivel chairs. It probably hadn't had a face-lift in sixty years.

Roman, a strapping young Amish man a few years younger than Gideon, looked up from his wheelchair. "Finally, a customer!" He grinned. "Aden's been cooking since four this morning. But it looks like the weekend following Thanksgiving Day is going to be slow this year. What can we get for you, Gideon?"

Aden, Roman's identical twin, gave Gideon a brief nod as he stood at the sink, washing pots and pans.

"I'll take the house special." Gideon wasn't hungry, but how could he fail to support a diner that was so rural it had almost no business on the busiest shopping weekend of the year? The Hertzlers' store stayed covered with customers on days like this, but Zook's sat in the middle of nothing, ten miles away. "Five of them, to go."

"Now we're talking." Roman wheeled himself to the take-out containers and placed five of them in his lap. Aden went to the icebox and pulled out a carton of eggs.

Gideon figured he could drop off the breakfasts at the Snyder place, where the crew of six men were trying to get the house dried in. Even though some were bound to have eaten already, they would still devour these breakfasts in no time.

"Aden, I have a proposition for you."

Roman looked to Aden and then to Gideon. "What is it?"

Since Aden struggled with a stutter, Roman did most of the talking for him. Gideon wasn't sure whether Aden liked it that way or the outgoing and talkative Roman just never gave his brother a chance to speak. But whatever the dynamics of that relationship, Aden stayed in the shadows, cooking, and Roman waited tables and charmed customers. But Aden's real skill wasn't as a short-order cook. He was a quite talented artist.

Gideon pulled his billfold out of his pants pocket. "Remember when you drew some sketches of cakes for Mattie's portfolio?"

Aden gave a lopsided grin. "Y-ya."

"You heard about her cake shop burning down, right? And that she's come home for a bit?"

"We heard," Roman said. "Is she doing all right?"

He wasn't so sure she was. "Considering everything, ya, I think so. But the portfolio, which she's been adding to since she was a kid, burned in the fire."

Aden stopped scrambling the eggs. "I'm sor- sor-"

"Ya," Roman interrupted. "He's sorry to hear that. We both are."

Aden flashed a look from Roman to Gideon. Roman nodded. "Oh, ya. So what can he do for you?"

Gideon rested his forearms on the counter. "I was hoping you could remember some of the things you drew, and anything else you remember seeing in her portfolio, and would draw them again fresh."

"Sure," Roman said. "He'd be glad to. I bet he remembers

everything he saw in that book, but it's been a while since he looked at it."

"I'm pretty familiar with what all was in there, so I might be some help."

He'd looked at her portfolio several times since they'd gone their separate ways—not that Mattie had a clue. Her brother James did, as well as Dorothy. But he was confident neither of them had ever mentioned his visits to Mattie. She didn't want to know anything about him, and they respected that. He had no desire to alter the course of her life, but in his pitiful stabs at protecting her, he couldn't help but keep up with her life.

Roman rolled his wheelchair out of the kitchen, carrying five takeout boxes stacked on top of one another. "Why don't you give him a few days and then you two get together and take a look at what he's got?" Roman went to the cash register and rang up the food items.

"If that sounds good to you, Aden, that's what we'll do."

Aden nodded.

Gideon passed Roman two twenties.

"What I don't get is why you're helping her out. You two ended things years ago—and not on very pleasant terms." Roman grabbed a roll of quarters and broke them open into the change drawer.

"Sometimes a man needs to redeem his past. And for the

record, this transaction is just between us. When the portfolio is complete, Aden, you can take it or mail it to her, and leave my name out of it." He eyed the talkative one. "Okay, Roman?"

"People always think I share everything I know." He counted out the change and passed it to Gideon. "I can keep a secret just as well as my brother." Roman pulled bills out of the register and laid them on the shelf above the cash drawer. "Just you—"As the door to the restaurant opened, he dropped his sentence and froze in place.

Gideon turned to see the distraction. A young woman stepped inside, carrying what appeared to be a very heavy cardboard box. She looked a little familiar, but Gideon couldn't place her. Her small, circular prayer Kapp and her flowery blue cape dress that showed below her heavy coat told him she belonged to the Old Order Mennonite sect.

He glanced at Roman and saw insecurity in his eyes, erasing all hints of his outgoing personality. He backed his wheelchair away from the cash register.

Gideon looked at Aden, and his usual lack of confidence faded as he caught her eye. Smiling, Aden came out of the kitchen and walked directly toward her.

"Morning, Aden." She returned his smile.

Aden took the box, his eyes fixed on hers. "M-m-morning, Annie."

Clearly, Aden didn't want Roman speaking for him when it came to this young woman.

She lowered her head, a pink blush rising in her cheeks before she peered around him. "Hello, Roman."

Roman's fingers tightened on the hand rim of his wheelchair. "Is something wrong with Moses?"

Now Gideon remembered who she was—one of Moses Burkholder's granddaughters. She didn't live in Apple Ridge, but she came here when her *Daadi* Moses needed her.

She took off her coat. "He's down with bronchitis, but the doctor says he'll be fine in a week or two."

Moses was a silent partner in the diner. Without him, the Zooks would have lost their family restaurant. Aden and Roman's grandfather had built this place years ago and had run it without electricity. When regulators mandated that electricity had to be installed to meet new legal codes, Moses stepped in and became a partner. Members of the Old Order Amish church couldn't have a business with electricity, but they could co-own a place with a Plain Mennonite, who could have electricity installed.

Gideon pondered the opposite reactions the Zook twins had to Annie. Of all the Old Order Amish and Old Order Mennonites he'd known, he'd never heard of anyone crossing the line from one sect to the other—not even to court, much less marry. It was forbidden, and if one of them was interested in her, it could cause a rift between her grandfather and the Zooks, perhaps destroying the family business as well as the years of trust between them.

If Gideon understood anything about love between a man and a woman, he knew it could grow where it wasn't planted and thrive without anyone nurturing it—like poison ivy. And it could make a man just as miserably uncomfortable.

"Roman." Gideon nodded toward the cash.

"Oh, ya." He passed him the money.

Gideon shoved it into his pocket, grabbed the takeout boxes, and said good-bye.

Regardless of what was going on with these three, Gideon had his own battle to focus on—the one of avoiding Mattie Lane.

Mattie sat in Beth's office at Hertzlers' Dry Goods, using the community phone to make calls. If Mattie used the phone shanty at home, Mamm would fix her a favorite meal or start making her a new dress. Whenever Mattie was doing business on their property, Mamm was on the move. So each time Mattie thought of someone who'd ordered a cake from Mattie Cakes, she came here to call them and let them know she was out of business, probably until April. She wished she had a better way of reaching everyone, because relying solely on her memory could cause someone not to be ready for a big event.

Once a piece of information concerning a client came to her—like an address, a relative's name, or a husband's first name—she called directory assistance to get the phone number. She dialed Mrs. Gibbons, an Englischer who'd ordered a cake for her parents' sixtieth anniversary. This was Mattie's third phone call of the day, and each one was difficult to get through. She explained the situation to her, and just like all the others she'd spoken to, Mrs. Gibbons was kind in accepting that she couldn't fill the order. But every client asked what caused the fire. When she explained she'd left the place unattended with papers near the wood stove, they seemed satisfied with the answer. What she didn't tell them was that in her pleasure at seeing Ryan's excitement over his cake, she might have laid her notebook on the wood stove before leaving the store for more than an hour.

Being creative was fun. But for her the flip side of creativity was being scattered, and she *really* didn't enjoy that part.

Lizzy quietly slipped into the room and went to a file cabinet. Mattie finished her phone call and put the receiver in its cradle. "Seems to me the more you add on to this store, the busier you get. You're not getting ahead, Aunt Lizzy."

"I said the same thing the other day," she teased.

Her aunt always seemed to look a decade younger than she was, but now she absolutely glowed. Lizzy's dark hair had very few strands of gray, and her sparkling brown eyes said she'd never been happier. Mattie wondered how amazing it must feel to be forty and getting married for the first time.

Maybe she would be that happy by the time she reached forty. It felt as if it'd take that long, anyway.

She caught a glimpse of movement across the yard and glanced that way.

Gideon.

She'd once loved him—his energy, his sense of humor, his dedication to God, family, and work.

He had a stack of two-by-fours on one shoulder and a huge bucket of paint, maybe twenty gallons, in his free hand, carrying them as if they were no heavier than an umbrella.

Beiler Construction belonged to Gideon's grandfather and then to his Daed, who had several sons, but the business was in serious financial trouble by the time Gideon graduated from school at twelve. Even as a scrawny kid, he poured his energy and heart into the business, as did his brothers. By the time he turned seventeen, no worker was more powerful or capable.

Over the years she and Gideon had discovered some of the problems Beiler Construction had with supplies, contracted labor, and scheduling projects. She'd cherished those times of talking over business issues while on a date or sharing a meal with his family. She had come up with some helpful solutions, and it'd made her feel valuable to him. And to his family.

But somewhere along the way, Gideon decided that she didn't mean enough to him.

Lizzy followed her gaze. "Is something wrong?"

Mattie cleared her throat, trying to think of a cover. "Just wondering if the house will be done in time." That was true enough, wasn't it?

"I'm sure it'll be done sufficiently."

Wondering what had caused Gideon to change his mind about her was a subject she'd put away a long time ago, and she refused to start rehashing it now. As long as she was on this earth, she wouldn't know the answers to lots of things, and that was one of them.

"Do you have pictures of the types of cakes you're making these days?"

Mattie shook her head. "When I find something similar, I'll show it to you. With the big day in two weeks, I have no time to lose." She didn't even have the right cake pans for what she hoped to make for her aunt.

"I don't want anything fancy," Lizzy said. "But I'd like it to be memorable."

Mattie suppressed a smile. She heard this sentiment regularly when making cakes for the Amish. "I'll do just that. And I want your cake to be quite different from Beth's. What did you have in mind?"

"Omar's eyes always light up when people have one of those enormous cakes like you made for your parents' anniversary a few years ago. I was going to try to make it myself, but since you're here, I'll gladly turn that responsibility over to you. Is it possible to make one like that?"

"Unfortunately, that large pan was charred and warped in the fire. I could bake several smaller ones and put them together."

Lizzy frowned. "You can't keep doing that forever. You need new pans. If you'll order them, I'll be glad to pay for them."

"I can't let you do that."

"You most certainly can, and I'll not hear another word about it, or I'll go straight to the bishop."

Mattie laughed. "You're going to take full advantage of marrying the bishop, aren't you?"

Lizzy moved around to Mattie's side of the desk. She cupped Mattie's face in her hands. "Seriously, let us replace those pans."

She'd forgotten how pleasant it was to be treated special by Lizzy. "Denki."

"So where do we buy them?"

"I don't know." Gideon had special-ordered them from a

man who'd never made cake pans before. All she had to do was find the courage to ask Gideon for the man's name and number. "I'll see what I can find out."

"Sounds good to me. I need to get back to work, and you need to get busy finding some answers."

"Denki, Lizzy."

"It's good to have you back, Mattie." She closed the door behind her.

Mattie didn't want to ask Gideon for help, but she couldn't afford to lose time searching for someone else to make the pans. She put on her coat and walked onto the main floor of the dry goods store.

"Hey." Beth stopped sorting books. "You leaving?"

"I need to ask Gideon a question, and if he has an answer, I may need to use your phone again. I'm trying to avoid doing business at home because Mamm stays on her feet the whole time."

"Come back whenever you need to. If the store is closed, just bang on the door. I'll hear you."

"I'm sure you're looking forward to living somewhere other than above this store."

"I'm looking forward to getting married." She raised her eyebrows. "Where we live isn't that important right now."

Mattie laughed. "Must be nice." She waved. "I hope to see

you in just a bit." She left the store and walked across the parking lot and the lawn and into Beth's new home. "Hello?"

"In the kitchen," Gideon groaned.

When Mattie walked in, he had a large kitchen cabinet balanced between the wall and his shoulder. One hand was stretched up as high as he could reach on the front of the cabinet, his face was turning red, and his arms were shaking.

"Could you do me a favor?"

His predicament and his nonchalant question didn't exactly match, and she found it quite amusing. It was obvious her answer needed to be yes, but something playful in her, or maybe the need to aggravate him, came out of hiding. "Maybe."

"Mattie Lane," he growled.

She laughed. "Well, what is it?"

He nodded toward the floor, and she noticed a broken deadman brace. "There's another one on the back porch." He gritted his teeth under the weight of the cabinet.

She ran to get it and hurried back. She propped the T of it as he'd shown her years ago. Then she crawled onto the makeshift countertop and helped hoist the cabinet into place and held it steady while he got one nail in—hopefully into a stud, or the cabinet would fall.

She closed her eyes while the hammer banged away.

"We did it." Gideon rubbed his shoulder. "That'll keep it

from falling while I get the screws in." He offered her a hand down.

She hesitated, confusion churning. Taking his hand could be a mistake, one that might unleash thoughts and feelings she couldn't allow. She shooed him away and hopped down. "Where's your helper?"

"The crews are at another home, trying to get it dried in before bad weather hits." He used his level to get the cabinet just right, and then with a battery-powered screwdriver, he sank two long screws into the cabinet and wall.

"The business must really be behind schedule."

"Might be the worst yet." He removed the brace and set it aside.

Memories of their brainstorming about scheduling issues stung her heart for a moment. She'd loved those times—looking for solutions, laughing at some of the ridiculous predicaments Beiler Construction dealt with, and letting him vent his frustrations. Apparently he hadn't felt the same way.

Mattie rubbed her hands together, trying to warm them. "Why are you installing cabinets anyway? Does Beiler Construction do that now?"

"No. That's why this cabinet job wasn't likely to go well no matter how many hands were here. But my oldest brother decides who'll be where these days."

"John? That's your position. You earned it."

He shrugged, obviously not interested in talking about John taking over as the lead contractor of Beiler Construction. He dusted off his shirt. "Denki for your help, Mattie. If I'd tried to set the cabinet down, it would've toppled and gotten damaged, and I couldn't keep holding it up."

She dropped the subject of John. It wasn't any of her business who was the walking boss of Beiler Construction, but if Gideon were running it, no one would be finishing a job by himself.

He folded his arms, leaned against the counter, and narrowed his eyes at her. "I was in a bind and asked for help, and your answer was 'maybe'?"

She barely managed to keep the grin off her face. "It was tempting to see how long you could last. When you said you needed a favor, it was all I could do not to ask, 'Now?' "

The amusement in his eyes made her long for the days when she was the one who'd mattered most to him. Uncomfortable with her thoughts, her mirth vanished.

She pulled a scrap of paper out of her coat pocket and laid it on the counter. "The reason I'm here is to ask if you have the name and number of the man who made those custom-sized pans for me."

"Ya." He pulled out the tape measure and started working again.

"May I have it?"

"Now?"

She resisted laughing. "No. I could wait until you're asleep tonight and toss a rock through your window."

"Again?" He mocked gaping at her. "Didn't we get into enough trouble the first time?"

"Uh, I didn't get into trouble. Only you did. Actually, I think my Daed was quite proud that his only daughter could throw a rock that far and that hard at twelve years old."

"What was the deal with you throwing a rock and me getting in trouble for it? I was asleep!"

"Mammi Beiler said it had to be your idea, and since you were older, I was totally under your influence."

"Whatever," he teased.

Her heart pounded, enjoying the nostalgia they so easily shared. She reminded herself of who he was and cleared her throat. "The man's name and number?"

"Sure. Dennis Ogletree. I met him on a job site one time, and we've stayed in contact. He's a machinist by trade. He can make the pans in less than a day once he gets to the project. I'm just glad to see a spark of life returning to your face."

"Do not say the word *spark* to me, please."

His familiar lopsided smile that held more compassion than humor sent fear running through her. Getting along with women came effortlessly to him, and she was a fool to be drawn in so easily.

A hint of a thought darted across his face before he took a wristwatch out of his pants pocket and glanced at it. He grabbed a carpenter's pencil off the countertop.

While he wrote down the information, she noticed a small bucket filled with a bundle of fall flowers sitting on the floor near the washroom. Since it was the end of November, they had to come from a florist.

"Aw, Beth's getting flowers from Jonah. How sweet."

He glanced up, his face flushed. She hadn't meant anything by her observation, but he certainly seemed uncomfortable.

He slid the paper across the counter toward her. "You should go call him now."

"You think he's home in the middle of the day?"

"You won't know until you try." He gestured toward the door, clearly trying to hurry her along.

She studied the measurements he'd jotted down under the name and phone number. "Are these the size pans I should order?"

"It's what I ordered before."

"Denki." She put the paper into her pocket while going toward the door.

"No problem."

When she went outside, she saw a car pull up near the house. She continued down the steps and toward the store. The driver tooted the horn and hopped out. She had short black hair and wore dangly gold earrings and a bright red sweater with a yellow and red scarf. She was stunning, and Mattie couldn't help but think that she strongly resembled the girl Mattie had caught Gideon with three years ago. But she was too young to be Ashley.

"Is Gideon here?" she asked Mattie.

His desire to hurry her out the door suddenly made perfect sense. He didn't want her to know he was still seeing Englischer girls. She'd kept her mouth shut about it when they broke up. Did he think she'd make trouble for him now by telling the church leaders or his family? It was broad daylight, and he wasn't exactly sneaking around, so people had to know, didn't they? "He's inside."

The girl reached in and tooted the horn again. He came out onto the porch, the container of flowers in hand.

"Oh, they're beautiful!" She scurried up the steps and threw her arms around his neck.

Mattie's eyes caught Gideon's, and she wondered if he had any idea how disappointing his behavior was. Would he ever mature and either join the faith or leave it? And would she ever grow out of caring?

Eight

*G*ideon got into Sabrina's car. She maneuvered the flowers as she climbed behind the wheel, then passed them to him and started the engine. Soon they were pulling onto the road.

The look in Mattie Lane's eyes made him want to slither away. Living a lie was so much easier when she wasn't here to see him. If his life had gone down the path he'd expected, she would have understood the reason for what he did to her, and she would have forgiven him.

Sabrina held out her hand, palm up. "We don't see each other often enough."

He put his hand in hers and squeezed it before letting go.

"So who was the cute blond chick?"

"Chick?" He tried to sound jovial. "Is your generation using that word now?"

"My generation? You're not that old."

He couldn't think of one humorous thing to say, and he only had the energy to be honest. "I feel old."

"Yeah, Ashley used to say that too."

Weariness engulfed Gideon as he remembered his friend.

Sabrina pulled into the cemetery and parked the car. "I can't believe it's been two years." She gripped the steering wheel and stared at the headstones. "It's so unfair."

He got out and went around to her side of the vehicle. After opening her door, he passed her the flowers. "Kumm."

They ambled through the beige grass, and dried leaves crunched under their feet. When they came to Ashley's headstone, Sabrina removed an old arrangement and replaced it with the new one. "We didn't forget you." She brushed her fingertips along the top of the headstone. "We'll never forget," she whispered. She moved to Gideon's side and wrapped her arms around him. "Do you still miss my sister?"

"Not the same way you do, but ya."

"Nothing was ever the same after she was diagnosed."

He squeezed her tight. Even now, in spite of how much they'd talked about Ashley and her painful journey, Sabrina couldn't manage to say the word *leukemia*. "How's your family?"

"Coping better, but a piece of everyone who loved her died when she did."

"I know."

His heart had never been heavier.

If he explained his motives and reasoning to Mattie for what he did, she'd feel differently, and maybe she'd regain a tiny measure of respect for him. But he wouldn't do it. He refused to chance opening a door for her to return...or to risk watching her learn the truth and then not come back to him.

Sabrina tugged on his coat. "Come on. I'll let you buy me lunch at Zook's."

The weathered headstones stood stark and lonely as he and Sabrina drove toward the exit, and suddenly he was filled with a desire to grab on to life while he still could. But such longings weren't meant for people with a death sentence. What could be gained by reaching for something he couldn't hold on to?

Even as he asked himself that question, he knew the truth— he didn't want to take hold of something for forever. Only God knew how many days he had on this earth. Gideon trusted Him with the keeping of every sunrise, sunset, and all that was in between. He trusted Him concerning every battle, and he knew the power of the Cross. Those were the big issues, and Gideon had peace concerning his days and the end of them, but that aside, he still craved one thing—a little time with Mattie.

Sol stood in the tiny shed he called a workshop, behind his Daed's house, hammering out his frustrations by attaching stringers to yet another pallet. But his mind wasn't on the work. His thoughts lingered on Mattie…or, more accurately, on what Katie King had told him yesterday about her.

Mattie had been gone less than a week, and he felt all out of sorts. Displaced, he guessed. He had to talk to her, if just to regain his bearings. Yesterday he'd gone to King's Harness Shop to use their phone and call her at her Mamm's. But no one answered.

While he was there, Katie had braved the cold winds to walk from her house to her Daed's shop so she could tell him some news about Mattie.

"I was helping Daed, and I couldn't help but overhear the conversation when James Eash stopped by to call his mother." Katie had smoothed her dress time and again. "In response to something his Mamm said, James said it was hard to believe that Mattie and Gideon were able to work in the same house together."

When she'd said those words, Sol had felt a storm of emotions he couldn't begin to decipher.

"That struck me as an odd conversation. I know I've heard James mention that name before, but I don't know who Gideon is. Do you know him?"

After swallowing hard, Sol had said, "We've met."

"James also said he wasn't surprised that Gideon was doing whatever he could to help her replace all her pans."

Sol's jumbled emotions had funneled into one: irritation. First the man broke her heart, and then when she was clearly in a relationship with someone else, he decided to treat her right. "Maybe I should visit Mattie…make sure she's doing okay."

"That's sweet, Sol."

"I hope I can find a driver on such short notice."

"You know, my family's going to Lancaster tomorrow. Daed has some business there, and the rest of the family is going to visit relatives. We have to go through Apple Ridge on the way."

"Think your Daed would mind if I hitched a ride with you and your family?"

She'd grinned. "I know he won't. He's got an order to drop off at your Daed's place. He could do that tomorrow and pick you up while he's there."

Tired of replaying yesterday's events over and over, Sol put another board on the pallet and nailed it into place. There was no way Mattie would get involved with Gideon again.

Was there?

Through the tiny window of the shed, Sol saw a large white van pull into his Daed's driveway. The driver turned off the engine and leaned back, waiting for his passengers to disembark.

Benuel King, Katie's Daed, got out of the van, and his wife and five children followed suit. Sol's father came out of the house, and the two men opened the back of the van and pulled out two leather horse collars and the rigging, which they carried to the barn. Katie's Mamm and four siblings went inside the house with Sol's mother.

Katie stood on the driveway, looking at him through the shed window. She pointed at herself and then his shed, asking if he minded her coming over. He hesitated but motioned to her. He didn't want to talk with her, but she didn't make him as nervous today, probably because he was in too foul a mood to care what she thought.

Katie meandered into the shed, her brown eyes studying every inch of the small room. "Do you always work with the doors open and the kerosene heater running in winter?"

He put the unfinished pallet under the workbench. "Most of the time," he mumbled.

"You don't like being closed in, do you?"

He hadn't thought about it, but she was right. He shrugged rather than answer.

Katie shoved her hands into her coat pockets. "I shouldn't have said anything to you about what I overheard James saying on the phone. I feel like such a gossip."

"Why *did* you tell me?" Sol put his hammer on its peg to avoid looking at her.

"When Mattie first moved here, the single men went wild,

all wanting a chance with the new girl. But it was obvious to me that she had her sights on you."

Katie made him sound as if he were a buck grazing in an open field and Mattie had bagged him. He turned to her. "You sound jealous."

She froze for a moment, and he could see remorse reflected in her eyes. "It's true. I have been for so long, I guess I jumped at the first chance to make you see her in a bad light." She closed the gap between them. "But I'm not a bad person, Sol. I'm not jealous because of her success or because she turned the heads of all the other guys. What bothers me is that you started talking to me before she butted in. After that, you never even noticed me."

Three years ago it never dawned on him that Katie was interested in him. He'd thought she was just being her silly self, talking about nothing. Seemed odd she'd still be miffed about that, but he wasn't interested—not then or now. "I'm sorry. I didn't realize you felt that way."

"Are you upset with Mattie over what I told you?"

"I'm not going to Apple Ridge because of some one-sided piece of a conversation you overheard. I just want to visit her." He looked at Katie, realizing he no longer was the bundle of insecurity he'd always been around girls. For the first time he didn't feel nervous and miserable. He felt confident, just as he did when sitting in Mattie's cake shop talking to her.

He saw their Daeds returning from the barn and walked toward the door.

Katie grabbed the sleeve of his coat. "You let her hold too much power over you."

Sol gently pulled her hand free of his coat. "You don't look so good in green, Katie."

Mattie hitched her Daed's horse to a carriage and led the old girl to her front door. "Wait right here." She patted Jessie Bell's head and hurried into the kitchen to grab her sample cakes and head for Beth's.

Mamm stood at the table, wiping it down.

"Mamm, it's clean. Go rest." Mattie kissed her cheek. "Please."

"There's something sticky." Mamm scrubbed a spot as if trying to remove tar. Her gray hair had lost its luster long ago, and her pale skin had deep lines. She didn't need to stay in the kitchen the whole time Mattie was baking, but Mamm wouldn't have it any other way.

Mamm had gotten up with her before dawn this morning, helping her look through the stack of cake magazines Mackenzie had sent with her. The glossy pages had all sorts of pictures of wedding cakes, and they'd poured hours into looking through them and flagging the ones to show Beth and Lizzy. None of the images quite matched what Mattie wanted to make for them, but it would give the brides-to-be a few ideas so she could begin to make plans.

Mamm had stayed by her side while she prepared four types of cakes and frostings. Mattie intended to surprise Lizzy, Beth, and Jonah with samples of flavors she could make for their big day. She planned on stopping by Omar's on her way to the store to see if he could come to this surprise tasting too.

Taste-testing events were fun. The couples tended to enjoy each flavor of cake and frosting. But then they had to keep tasting and talking about the cakes until they could decide which one was their favorite.

She'd made Beth and Lizzy each a cake from a favorite flavor of theirs, then she'd added Belgian chocolate and buttercream filling to one and chocolate ganache with vanilla pastry-cream filling to the other. After that she made two cakes from flavors that were a bit more romantic in her estimation— an orange coconut cake with orange syrup and buttercream icing, and an apricot-praline cake with Bavarian cream filling.

Mamm had watched, cleaned up after her, and even offered suggestions, but she didn't have the energy to keep up with someone Mattie's age.

When Mamm stopped scrubbing her table, Mattie took the rag from her and put it in the sink. "Kumm." She took her by the hand and led her into the living room. "You prop up your feet and read awhile, okay?"

Mattie counted each year that her Mamm lived as a blessing, one she never took for granted. But sometimes they were too close for their own good. Moving away after she and Gideon had broken up hadn't been easy, but it'd been good for both of them.

Mamm had nearly died when Mattie was sixteen. She'd spent months in the hospital, battling lupus, and she'd had some close calls after that. At the time, Mattie had stopped everything to become her caretaker. But Mamm had slowly regained her strength, and she'd been holding her own since then.

Mamm slapped the arms of the chair. "Oh, I should go to the grocery store and get more supplies for you while you're at Beth's."

"You've done plenty. I'll get whatever we need." She didn't know how to handle the next few weeks where she'd need days of long hours to get Beth's and Lizzy's cakes made, but working in Mamm's kitchen wasn't the answer.

"Mattie," Mamm fussed, "the grocer is in the opposite direction of Hertzlers'."

"I know that, and I'm fine." She passed her a paperback book. "Promise me you'll rest."

Mamm's blue eyes stayed steady on her. "You're the one who was injured. And you're dealing with the shock of your shop burning."

Mattie sat on the ottoman near Mamm's feet. "Look me in the eyes. Do I appear to be falling apart?"

She shook her head. "No, but I heard you crying a few times after you crawled into bed."

"But the busier I stay, the better I feel, as long as I know I'm not wearing you out while I do it, okay?"

"You're sure you don't need me to—"

"I'm positive. What I need is for you to trust me."

Mamm patted her knee. "You always were a sweetheart."

"You too." Mattie squeezed her hand and returned to the kitchen.

She grabbed her mother's four cake carriers before getting into her carriage and heading to Hertzlers' Dry Goods. She'd ordered the pans from Mr. Ogletree Saturday evening, and he'd said she could pick them up at Lizzy's place after lunch today. So Beth and Lizzy were expecting her, which was good, but the cake-tasting venture would be a complete surprise.

Nine

A few hours after the deliverymen installed the gas-
powered refrigerator and oven, Gideon finished hanging the last door. His joints ached, and a bone tiredness that he
hadn't experienced in a long time wearied him. Maybe he was
pushing himself too hard to finish this house, or maybe his
symptoms were recurring. He'd beaten all the odds, and every
routine medical test said he'd been clear of cancer for more than
a year, but his kind of leukemia could come back at any time
without warning.

Refusing to walk in fear, he whispered prayers of trust.
Minutes ticked by, and Gideon began singing praises to God.
Soon the aches stopped looming like a huge monster. Peace settled over him, and he was able to concentrate on the work at
hand.

The cabinets and countertops were in place, and yesterday
the heating guy had put in the wood furnace in the basement.
The plumber would be here tomorrow to add the faucets and

commodes and hook up the water. Gideon still had a pretty long to-do list, but he'd accomplished a lot in the last couple of days.

After leaving the cemetery with Sabrina, he'd squashed the desire for a little time with Mattie and had dived into work…as he'd always done when he had the strength. But working like crazy wasn't enough this time. He wanted to be with her today more than he wanted a promise of life tomorrow.

Conversations filtered into the master bedroom. It sounded as if three or four people had entered the front door.

"Oh, just look at this place!" Beth exclaimed. "Gideon?"

He walked down the hallway to the kitchen.

Jonah peeled out of his coat. "We have heat."

Beth, Jonah, Lizzy, Omar, and Mattie Lane were taking off their jackets. Mattie set a large paper bag with handles on the counter. Beth turned toward him. "How have you gotten so much done since I was here yesterday?"

"He's barely slept," Jonah offered.

Without looking at Gideon, Mattie reached into the bag she'd brought.

"Seems like his loss is your gain." Omar winked at Beth.

At times like these, Gideon was glad Bishop Omar didn't know his secret. But living a lie was exhausting.

"Kumm." Beth motioned for him. "Mattie made samples of wedding cakes, and I wanted to taste them in our new home. You have to try these and help us decide."

"Maybe he has other plans." Mattie shot him a quick look. "Ones that don't include hanging out with Plain old us."

He looked at the others to see if they had caught her barbed meaning, but they seemed too interested in the cakes. Clearly she was disappointed in him for leaving with an Englischer girl the other day. She probably wished he'd leave again, but his stubborn side refused to give her what she wanted.

Mattie pulled a small spiral notebook out of the bag, and her eyes grew large. She looked straight at him, as she had so many times in the past. At this moment she seemed void of anger, and it moved him.

"Missing something?" he asked.

"I didn't think to bring plates."

"I'll go get some from my place," Lizzy said. She and Omar put on their coats and hurried out the door.

Mattie set the notebook on the counter, pulled out a cake carrier, and looked into the bag again. Lines creased her face. "I didn't bring napkins either."

"The store has rolls of paper towels." Beth grabbed her coat. "I'll be right back."

"Thanks." Mattie turned to Gideon. "Can we start a fire in the hearth? You know, for a more special atmosphere."

"Sure. It's got a gas starter." Gideon went to the woodbin.

"Oh, no. Beth, wait."

Gideon turned to see Mattie hurrying to the door, trying to catch Beth, but she was halfway across the parking lot.

"What else did you forget?" Jonah asked.

"Forks to eat with and a knife to cut the cakes."

Jonah went to the door and then paused. "Anything else?"

She rolled her eyes. "Look, I've never done one of these outside my shop, and I had all this stuff there."

Moving logs to the fireplace, Gideon chuckled. "This is why I call her Mattie Lane. A day with her is a journey all by itself—a trip down a one-of-a-kind country road."

She gave Jonah an apologetic shrug. "I guess I am Mattie Lane after all."

Jonah laughed. "I'll be right back."

The house became quiet again. Gideon turned on the gas and lit a flame under the logs. He dusted off his hands and stood. "Did you remember the cakes?"

"Of course." She held up a cake carrier and frowned. "Wait. I…I only have one. What'd I do with the other three?" She looked into the paper bag. "I know I loaded four cake carriers in Mamm's kitchen. How could I not have them?"

"Because when you're on Mattie Lane, magical things happen."

She pursed her lips. "I don't like that lane, and clearly you don't either. I don't want to pull everyone else along that path with me."

He wanted to tell her that he'd always loved being a part of her world. But if he did, he'd have to explain why he'd broken up with her. "Maybe they're in the rig."

Her eyes lit up. "Ya, maybe." She put on her coat, then looked at him with concern. "What if I put the cake carriers on the carriage's sideboard when I left Mamm's? They'll be scattered all over the road."

"One step at a time, Mattie Lane. Kumm." He opened the door for her, and they went to the hitching post. The air smelled of snow, and a car parked at Hertzlers' Dry Goods had a pine tree strapped to its roof, reminding him that Christmas was less than a month away. The weeks leading up to Christmas always went by so quickly, as if a week equaled one day instead of seven. He wished that by some Christmas miracle time would slow and these days with Mattie nearby would last forever.

They went to the passenger side, and he opened the door of the rig. "Oh, good." A beautiful grin removed all the stress from her face.

She grabbed two cake carriers and passed them to him and then took out the last one and slammed the door to the rig. "I drive myself crazy sometimes." She studied him. "Did my forgetfulness drive a wedge between us and I was too scattered to know it? You can tell me the truth."

He couldn't move. At the time he'd been so sure of himself,

confident of his decision to lie in order to free her. Now a glimpse of insight into what he'd done to her chipped away at his certainty. "No, Mattie. I promise."

Her blue eyes stayed glued to him, and his heart pounded.

"*Gut.*" She nodded and walked back to the house.

He followed, wondering if he should tell her the truth. She needed to be set free from thinking he hadn't cared for her, but how could he do that without revealing his deception? He always figured she'd understand one day. But her question of self-doubt haunted him.

Beth and Jonah returned, goods in hand. "Look." She held up a handmade Christmas card. "We've received our first card of the season. It's addressed to Jonah and me." She put it on the fireplace mantel before turning to Jonah, satisfaction and joy radiating from her.

Lizzy and Omar walked in, each carrying a small box of items. "Plates." Lizzy held them up. "We also brought mugs, coffee, and the fixings."

"Great." Mattie opened the carriers and doled out a slice of cake to everyone in the group. "This first sample is praline-and-apricot yellow cake with Bavarian cream filling." She handed a paper towel to each person.

"Oh, I love apricot yellow cake," Lizzy said.

The moans and aahs over how good it was made Mattie Lane smile.

"Isn't it delicious, Gideon?" Beth asked.

"Ya." He hated that his tone sounded flat, but no part of him cared about cake right now. He stood mesmerized and bewildered at all he felt for the one who'd made it.

"Denki." A slight smile graced her face. She put another type of cake on Beth's plate and then Lizzy's. "Next is strawberries-and-cream vanilla cake layered with vanilla pastry cream and chocolate ganache."

Beth dug her fork into it. "Oh, that is too good." She scooped up another bite and held it in front of Jonah.

He opened his mouth, and she gently fed it to him. "Incredible."

The happy couples gathered at the far end of the counter, talking about the different cakes and flipping through magazine cutouts in the spiral notebook. A few minutes later Mattie dished up the third type of cake, explained what it was, then added the fourth type, describing it also.

Beth, Jonah, Lizzy, and Omar moved into the living room, discussing the textures, colors, and flavors. Was this his opportunity to talk to Mattie alone for a few minutes?

"Your baking skills are even more impressive than I expected." Gideon hoped to relax her with some friendly conversation.

"Denki. Give a girl nothing but time to work on cakes, and it's amazing what she can accomplish."

Her response quickly stopped his effort at small talk.

Omar returned, holding up his plate. "Lizzy and I know which one we want."

Mattie wiped her hands on her apron and opened her notebook. "Which one?"

"The apricot-and-praline yellow cake with the Bavarian cream."

"Perfect." Mattie jotted down notes.

"We know too." Beth came in, licking her fork. "The strawberries-and-cream vanilla cake with the vanilla pastry-cream filling and the chocolate stuff."

"Ganache," Mattie said. "I thought you'd like that one."

Jonah pointed at his plate with his fork. "But that orange coconut cake with the buttercream icing is almost as delicious."

Mattie added notes about Jonah's second choice. "Got it. Denki."

"Look." Beth set down her empty plate as she gazed out the window. "It's snowing." She grabbed Jonah's and her coats. "Jonah, remember the year it snowed on Christmas Eve, stranding me at a motel, and you rescued me?"

Jonah grinned while putting on his coat. "Nope."

Beth laughed. "You do too." She took him by the hand. "Kumm." The back door slammed shut as they went outside.

Lizzy laughed. "Omar, do you mind if we join them?"

He held her coat while she slid her arms into it. "Of course not."

Lizzy turned to them. "Mattie, Gideon?"

"No, but denki." Mattie wiped her hands on her white apron again, watching Beth try to catch snowflakes in her hands. "I need to clean up."

Gideon shifted. "I think I'll get a bit more work done too."

Lizzy and Omar went out the back door.

Mattie focused on him, her light blue eyes reminding him of all they'd once shared.

Maybe he needed to address the Sabrina issue and put to rest her insecurity about why he broke up with her.

Gideon reached for his tool belt on the counter, then hesitated. "I think you need to know a few pieces of information I left out when we broke up." Even as he said that, he wondered just how much to tell her.

Mattie placed the leftover cake on a clean plate. "Seems to me it's long past time for you to clarify anything. But if you need some type of resolution, go ahead." Now that she'd concluded her cake-tasting event, her tone reflected what she really felt—like moving a pan from a cold back burner to a heated front one.

She handed him the roll of paper towels. Then she took the empty cake containers down the hall and stepped into the wash house.

He followed her, leaving the door open behind them. The almost-finished room had two mud sinks, a wringer washer, and a couple of stools.

Now that they were alone, all the reasons he'd broken up with her echoed in his mind. He silently prayed, hoping the right words would come to him.

Mattie Lane dumped the cake carriers into one of the sinks. "We actually get along pretty well when I manage to forget about your dating habits, although they are a little hard to block out when I'm face-to-face with the newest habit."

He stared at the paper towels in his hand. "That was Ashley's sister. Sabrina."

She wheeled around. "Gideon, how could you?"

"It's not like that, Mattie Lane. For one thing, I joined the faith two years ago and wouldn't go against our ways by dating outside the faith. Have you never asked anyone what I'm doing these days?"

"No," she snapped. "And the other thing?"

"Ashley died, and—"

She gasped. "I'm so sorry. What happened?"

"Leukemia."

Mattie's brow wrinkled. "How awful. I'm truly sorry."

"She had it when we met."

She peered at him, and he could see the light of understanding creep into her eyes. "Are you saying that you began to care for her…when she was sick?"

He shifted the paper towels into his other hand. "She was scared and needed a friend."

"So you ditched me?" Her eyes flashed. "You tossed me out like an old shoe?" She yanked a paper towel off the roll with such vengeance he nearly dropped it.

He knew when he'd used her jealous nature against her that she'd probably walk off and never look back. But now he needed her to understand he hadn't tossed her aside because he preferred someone else.

He rubbed the back of his neck. He should tell her he never thought of Ashley as more than a friend. But then what would he give as the reason he broke up with her? "The truth is—"

"Wait." She held up a hand. "Just because I happen to have crossed your path again, don't feel you need to make up a different story about what took place."

"I'm not doing that."

She wiped the cake carriers with a wad of towels, doing the best she could to clean without water. "The problem with liars and cheats is that they lose all credibility."

This was not going at all the way he'd hoped. Instead of his assuring her the breakup wasn't her fault, he was simply reopening old wounds.

Mattie finished scrubbing the cake carriers and set them in the sink. "I'm really sorry about Ashley," she said, her tone less harsh. "But at this point, I'm not sure you're even capable of telling me the truth."

"I am, Mattie Lane. With all my heart."

She tossed the frosting-covered paper towels into the second mud sink and looked up at him. "It's ridiculous, but I still want to believe you when you tell me something. But I can't. I just can't."

He avoided her steady gaze. "It won't do any good for me to try to explain if you're not going to believe me."

"I do believe you about Ashley." Her tone was typical Mattie Lane—a bit high-strung, yet tender-hearted and resolute. "And when I saw Sabrina, I noticed that she looked a lot like Ashley, so I believe you about her too."

That was a start. Gideon took a deep breath, wishing he could reveal the secret he'd been harboring. "I need you to know that our breakup had nothing to do with your not being good enough or perfect enough."

She scoffed. "Nearly three years after the fact, you're going to give me the line 'It wasn't you; it was me'? You must think I'm vulnerable and frail because my shop burned down."

"Don't be sarcastic. It doesn't suit you."

"Ya? Well, what does suit me, Gideon? Because whatever

it is, you suddenly seem to think it's your place to find out and fix it."

A van pulled up in front of Hertzlers' store, and a man got out. The lines of frustration faded from Mattie Lane's face. "Sol's here."

Once again, Mattie's beau showed up at an awkward time. "Were you expecting him?"

"He's supposed to be hunting." She pursed her lips together, suppressing a smile as she gazed out the picture window. "But whatever he's doing, I trust him in ways I thought I'd never trust again." She turned to Gideon. "Was there something else you wanted to tell me?"

He shook his head. "I suppose not."

She tucked a few stray strands of hair into her prayer Kapp and hurried out of the room.

Mattie still thought he'd fallen for Ashley and broken up with her because of it. The only thing this conversation had accomplished was that she knew he wasn't dating Sabrina.

He watched through the window as she slid into her coat while hurrying across the yard. Sol grinned and embraced her. Gideon's knees threatened to go weak on him, but he refused them that right.

Jonah tapped on the open door. "I saw Mattie out there. I suppose that's Sol."

"Ya."

"You doing okay?"

Gideon collapsed onto the stool in the corner of the wash house. "I wanted to tell her the truth."

Jonah closed the door. "What truth?"

Gideon rubbed clammy hands down his trousers. Even though he hadn't known Jonah much more than a year, he considered him a trustworthy friend. And it'd feel good to share his secret with someone. "Three years ago, in the fall, I started feeling strange. I was tired all the time, had night sweats, couldn't get rid of a cold, and spiked a high fever regularly for no apparent reason."

"Serious stuff."

"Ya. The first time I mentioned my symptoms to Mattie, she was alarmed, practically beside herself with concern, so I downplayed how I felt. Her mother has had health issues all of Mattie's life, and when she almost died about six years ago, Mattie struggled. She barely slept, and when she did, she had nightmares."

"Beth told me about that."

He scratched his brow, remembering how dark and confusing life was when he couldn't share his concerns with the one person he needed most. "After going in circles with doctors who couldn't figure out what was wrong, I went to a new doctor. He diagnosed me to be in the chronic phase of a rare form of leukemia." His throat closed up.

Jonah shifted his cane from one hand to the other. "I…I didn't know. "

"No one does, except my family, and I swore them to secrecy." He cleared his throat. "I told people I had out-of-town jobs, and I went to a cancer center in Philadelphia for treatment. That's where I met Ashley…Sabrina's sister. She'd had leukemia for years and was a volunteer at the clinic. We became friends. She believed we'd both get well, and I was almost convinced. But rather than me getting better, the cancer jumped to the worst possible stage—the blast phase."

"But you didn't tell Mattie what was going on?"

"I hated the idea of telling her. Still, I decided to tell her after the holidays. But on Christmas Day, Ashley came to my house, needing to talk. She'd received new test results, and her prognosis was grim. She'd been positive of a cure, regardless of the nightmare roller coaster she'd been on for so long. While I was consoling Ashley, Mattie walked in. She saw us hugging and wanted answers."

"What did you tell her?"

"That she needed to date others."

"Why would you say that?"

"Ashley's type of cancer was much easier to beat than mine,

and when her cancer returned, her whole family went into a tailspin. I knew I didn't want to drag Mattie down that road with me. Letting her think I cared for Ashley freed her to build a life of her own rather than watching mine deteriorate."

Jonah took the stool beside Gideon. "All this time you've let her believe you care for someone else?"

"I couldn't see any other way of protecting her...so I lied. I said I wanted to be free." But he hadn't been free. His heart had remained her captive. "Even though I'm in complete remission right now, the disease could return tomorrow. Or next year. Or a decade from now."

"Or never," Jonah took off his jacket. "You should've let Mattie make her own decision."

"She'd just turned nineteen the day before. A kid, really."

"And what were you, all of twenty-two?"

"Barely. I have no doubts that if she had known the truth, she would have stayed by my side." Gideon clenched his fingers together. "I'd never try to get her back. But watching her with someone else is killing me more than the cancer."

Jonah folded his hands together and stared at them. "Remember when you told me you found it odd that Beth, who's spent more than a decade making her own decisions, constantly asks my opinion about things?"

Gideon nodded. "You said that when two people are a couple, they need to get each other's opinions before making any decision that impacts both, or they'll store up trouble for their future."

"Regardless of the purity of your motivation, you've brought problems on Mattie and yourself."

Gideon shook his head. "I know I've hurt her. But staying with me would have brought her even more pain. There's no telling what it would have done to her."

"You think you were guarding Mattie's heart. But it sounds to me as if the only thing you protected her from was making her own choices."

Like a workhorse whose blinders had been removed, Gideon saw beyond the narrow path directly in front of him. He viewed a landscape that had once been fertile soil growing lush greenery but now was parched and desertlike with multiple shades of brown.

The cancer hadn't done that. He had.

And because of his actions, Mattie had moved away, found good soil, and replanted her life.

One question remained. What should he do now?

Ten

*A*fter embracing Sol, Mattie waited in the yard of Beth's home while he took his overnight bag to her carriage tied outside the store.

A light snowfall swirled around her, making everything look peaceful and charming, but Gideon's confession had rattled her. On the one hand, relief that he wasn't nearly as shallow as she'd thought lapped over her. On the other hand, disappointment that he'd chosen Ashley over her still stung—even if he had bonded with the Englischer girl out of compassion. At least his sketchy account of what had happened between the two of them lined up a lot better with who she'd always thought him to be, a kind and deeply caring man.

He should have told her the truth about Ashley *before* she caught them together. And when he broke up with her, why didn't he tell her about Ashley's illness? What had he been thinking?

Gideon had always been complicated. She used to think of

him like an oak tree—the magnificent, stretching limbs didn't compare to the complex root system.

Sol walked toward her, and she tried to clear her mind, not wanting Sol to see the conflicting emotions on her face. She wished she felt nothing for Gideon. But wishing it didn't make it real.

The man in front of her was the opposite of Gideon in every way. He said what he thought, always simple and straight-forward. She liked that about him. He wasn't full of twists and turns that could confuse or hurt her. She wished she could return to Ohio with him now and not look back. Since the cake-tasting was over, maybe she could pop back in and tell them a quick good-bye. Then she'd leave and keep right on moving…in every possible way.

She opened her arms, gesturing across the land. "Welcome to Apple Ridge."

"Denki." He glanced at the road. "I'm so glad you're here. Do you realize I don't have the address to your house?"

"So how did you find me?"

"The driver knew how to get to Hertzlers' Dry Goods, so our plan was to stop by and ask someone in the store where you lived. But here you are."

"I'm wrapping up a cake-tasting event for my cousin and aunt and their fiancés."

He placed his hands on her shoulders, looking bewildered, but his smile gave him away. "So how'd we manage two years of courtship without my ever coming to your folks' place?"

She put her arm around his waist, not feeling the least bit of warmth emanating from him through his wool coat. "Because they always visit us. And you would have been here for Thanksgiving this year...if the shop hadn't burned down. But you'll see my childhood home soon enough. Why don't you bring the rig up to the front door? I'll tell everyone a quick bye, and we'll be on our way."

He frowned, a moment of disbelief flashing in his eyes. "You don't want me to step inside and meet your cousin and aunt?"

Not really. She'd have to introduce him to Gideon, which would be awkward. But it'd only take a few moments. "Oh, ya. Sure." As they climbed the stairs to Beth's home, they parted a bit.

"Are you hungry?" she asked.

"No." He reached for her hand.

Holding hands was out of character for Sol, but she didn't question it. "Did I see other Amish in the van when you were dropped off?"

Lines of frustration showed on his face. "Ya. I rode with the King family. They're on their way to Lancaster. Since they have the only Amish community phone now that your cake shop is gone, I had to go there to call you, but no one answered at your folks' place."

"You could've used the phone at Mackenzie's store."

"Ya, then I'd be a spectacle to the Englischers. Besides, if I'd gone there, Katie wouldn't have told me that her family was coming through Apple Ridge so I could hitch a ride."

Guilt nibbled at Mattie's heart, and she couldn't manage to smile at him. While he'd been doing something very sweet by coming here, her thoughts were a tangled mess over Gideon. "That's quite a ride just to visit me."

"Ya. All I can say is I must be crazier about you than I realized. Hunting was no fun with you gone, and my nerves are raw from being closed up in a vehicle with her."

Her gut twisted with shame. He was being as straightforward and honest as ever, and she wanted to be like that for him too. She tugged on his hand. "Sol."

He stopped, and the sincerity in his eyes weighed heavily on her. She needed to at least brace him. "Gideon Beiler is inside."

His expression didn't change, but his gaze pierced her. "Inside the house? What's he doing here?"

"Working. He's the builder, and he's trying to finish it before their wedding."

He nodded and motioned toward the door. She reluctantly opened it, and they went inside.

Beth, Jonah, Lizzy, and Omar were in the kitchen, polishing off the cake crumbs on their plates. She introduced Sol around, and he shook each person's hand. When Gideon walked in, Sol stole a look at her. Her tongue was too thick to speak.

"We keep running into each other, Gideon." Sol shook his hand.

Gideon's jaw clenched. "Sol."

Confusion circled inside Mattie. "When did you two meet?"

"At the hospital the night you were injured." Sol said it casually while taking her hand in his again.

Mattie glanced from Gideon to Sol, aggravated that neither of them had told her. But this wasn't the time to talk about it.

"I hear you're a hunter," Jonah said. "Bagged anything of late?"

"Not really." Sol glanced at Gideon. "The woods are busy these days. When too many hunters crowd the same spot, no one goes home with anything."

Anger flashed in Gideon's eyes, but whatever he was thinking, he held his tongue.

Sol's veiled message hadn't bypassed anyone, and the room vibrated with discomfort. Embarrassment flushed Mattie's face. She wasn't some soft-eyed doe caught in Sol's cross hairs. She pulled her hand from his. "We need to go."

"Sure."

They said their good-byes and left the house. Mattie bit her tongue, determined not to say a word until they were in private. She strode across the lawn and the store's parking lot, removed the tether from the hitching post, and climbed into the rig. Sol got in beside her.

She took the reins and tapped them on the horse's back. "That was uncalled for."

"What?" He looked totally innocent.

"Comparing me to a deer. I'm not prized game, Sol."

"I don't think he picked up on it."

"Of course he did, and so did everyone else."

He shrugged. "I don't care."

"I do." When the horse flinched, she knew she needed to tone down her voice. "And why didn't you tell me Gideon came to the hospital?" She pulled out of the parking lot, taking a different route toward her home so they'd have time to settle this.

"You were under enough stress at the time without me adding something unimportant to you."

"Make up your mind. You didn't share it either because it'd be stressful for me or because you didn't think it mattered."

He stared out the frosty side window for several minutes. "Do you know what this is?"

"What?" she snapped.

"Our first argument." He propped his arm on the door of the carriage.

Until now she'd not thought about the fact that she and Sol never quarreled. She and Gideon had on numerous occasions. At various times they played, worked, and fought hard.

With passion and gusto—that's what Gideon used to call it. And then he'd smile, causing her heart to melt as he confessed that he wouldn't want it any other way…until Ashley came along.

Sol tapped his fingers on the fake wood on the dashboard. "Who is Gideon seeing these days?"

She shrugged. "I'm not sure."

"But you'd like to know."

"I didn't say that."

"True. But you didn't say, 'I don't care,' either."

She slowed the rig, pulling into a Mennonite church parking lot, and came to a halt. "I want to say it."

His features were lined with hurt. He scraped frost off the window with his fingernail. "You told me you let Gideon go because you refused to marry a man who had feelings for someone else. You wanted all or nothing. Remember us talking about that?"

"Ya."

"Here's the problem, Mattie. I feel the same way. I'm not

interested in making a big fuss if you have feelings for someone else."

"But I…I like who we are." Tears filled her eyes.

Sol cradled her face. "I do too. But your answer tells me I may have spent too much time thinking you're in love with me."

She pulled away, wiping her cheeks. "Are you breaking up with me?"

"No." He leaned back on the seat. "I hope that never happens." He brushed the back of his fingers down her face. "But I'd like you to sort out your feelings."

She tried not to gape at him. "Gideon's a cheater and a liar. You and I are good for each other."

"I think he regrets breaking up with you." Sol rubbed her tears off his fingers. The disappointment in his eyes cut her. "He beat me to the hospital when you were hurt, and he looked pretty shook up that night."

Her heart raced at the thought of losing Sol. "What are you saying?"

His amber eyes tugged at her heart. "I'll be in Ohio on Christmas Eve. I hope you'll be there for the singing. If not, we'll both know I'm not the one for you."

"I'll be there several days before then. I promise."

Eleven

With keys in hand, Gideon went up the stairs of Beth and Jonah's place.

Beth followed him, carrying a couple of bolts of fabric. "Sorry about coming by the Snyder place and interrupting your work. More than needing you to unlock the place, I don't want to walk across the floors until you verify they're dry enough for Mattie to get in here and work."

After finishing the floors, he'd purposely kept all the keys, trying to ensure that no one walked on the floors until they were dry. He slid the key into the deadbolt and turned it. When he opened the door, a strong smell of lacquer greeted him. Four days ago, two days after the cake tasting Sol had interrupted, he'd thoroughly cleaned the unfinished floors and then shellacked them. He'd locked up the house, leaving two windows slightly open, one in the wash house and one in the master bedroom. But that wasn't enough to disperse the smell.

At the time he did the floors, he hadn't known Mattie needed Beth's supersized oven to bake Lizzy's wedding cake.

He knelt before entering and pressed on the floor in different spots. "It's not the least bit tacky." He stood and motioned for her to go in ahead of him.

"Good." She stepped inside. "Sorry about the miscommunication. It never dawned on me that you were ready to do the floors this soon."

"It's not a problem for me, just for Mattie."

"She's been doing what she can from her home—making the fondants and preparing some of the smaller decorations. But her Mamm insists on helping, and Mattie doesn't want her to be on her feet much more. It'd be better if she can work here from now on."

Wondering if Sol was still in Apple Ridge, maybe even staying with Mattie's parents, Gideon put a key into Beth's hands. "You ladies can both come in and out as needed."

"Denki." She slid the key into her coat pocket and pulled out a sheet of paper. "This is a list of what I need to have done before the gathering."

While he read over it, Beth went down the hall and into the master bedroom.

"I think most of these things could wait a few days," he called out.

He really didn't want to spend time in the same house as Mattie, trying to protect the lie he'd told.

Maybe Jonah was right. Had he not protected Mattie at all? Still, telling her now was unacceptable. She and Sol were together, and he'd never do anything to change that.

But Jonah's words lay heavy across his shoulders, like a two-ton support beam that needed to be anchored in place, not toted around by a mortal man.

At the time of his lie, he'd considered it acceptable, even honorable—like Rahab, who betrayed her own city through a lie and brought favorable treatment to her whole family. Gideon had chosen to betray himself in order to open the door to good things for Mattie.

A lie would've been unacceptable if he'd wanted to get away with something for selfish purposes. But he hadn't profited from the lie. On the contrary, he'd paid dearly for it.

Beth walked back into the room, carrying the bolts of fabric. "What did you say?"

"I said I think I could wait on this list until after Lizzy's wedding."

Her lips hinted at a slight pout. "But Jonah's family is arriving at the end of the week, and I want everything comfortable for them. They'll be tired after coming all this way. I'd like to at least have all the shelves up in the closets and pantry, blinds or curtains on the windows, and gas night-lights installed so they don't hurt themselves if they get up in the dark." She held a piece of fabric near a window for a moment. "The pegs need to be made and inserted into the wainscot before Jonah's family arrives. And—"

"I read the list, Beth." Gideon lifted his tool belt off the countertop. "Go run your store. Or make curtains. Or something."

"Good idea." She took a few steps and stopped. "You will be nice to Mattie, won't you?"

Gideon chafed at the question. "Not a problem."

Beth pulled the door closed behind her.

He decided to start in the kitchen. Whatever he accomplished in adding shelves and such would make Mattie's preparation for the gathering easier. If he put in some extra hours now, he might get done and be out before she arrived.

Gideon had installed one shelf in the pantry when the front door opened. The sound of pans clattering to the floor indicated it wasn't Jonah. Gideon took a deep breath and went to the foyer. Stooping, Mattie gathered several pans.

He grabbed one, and she gasped, falling onto her backside. "Good grief." She got to her feet. "You startled me."

"Sorry, Mattie. I guess you couldn't hear me coming over the rattling of pans."

"Jonah said you were working on another job for a while."

"I was, but Beth came by with a list of items for me to finish."

Scowling, Mattie went into the kitchen. "Sounds like Beth and I need to talk. She can't expect us to work together like this."

"That's what I told her. But my protests fell on deaf ears." He picked up the rest of the pans and followed her. "Do you need help bringing more stuff in?"

"No. Whatever I managed to remember to bring, I can tote myself." She laid her small spiral notebook on the counter.

Gideon had seen Aden at Zook's Diner that morning and asked him about the drawings. He said he was nearly finished re-creating what he remembered. Gideon reminded him of some of the cakes she'd done that he knew about, and Aden promised to do his best to sketch them.

Mattie's countenance softened as she fiddled with the pages in the notebook. "I'm leaving for Ohio as soon as I can after Beth and Jonah's wedding." She lifted her eyes to his, and the sadness in them bothered him. "Whatever is happening between us here isn't good for me and Sol."

Gideon held her gaze, wishing he could have one day alone with her. Just one day to keep in his memory for the rest of his life. One day with no lies or anger or hurt between them—nothing except forgiveness and friendship.

"I understand." He cleared his throat, trying to make his voice sound normal. "I'll work in another room and leave you in peace."

He hung shelves in one closet after another. Hours passed, and the house smelled of cake and frosting, but Mattie Lane wasn't whistling. She used to whistle. Whenever he stopped making a racket, he heard her sigh and mumble.

A loud thud came from the front of the house, followed by a cry.

He rushed from the far end of the house into the kitchen. Mounds of frosted cake lay on the floor, and spatters of it clung to Mattie's face and dress.

She had her hands on her hips, and anger flashed in her eyes. "I lost all my cake stands in the fire. No one owns anything nearly large enough for a cake this size, so I tried making my own." She wiped cake off her face and pointed at the toppled stand. "I was sure it wouldn't break, but I didn't realize it was out of balance until I added the third layer."

"It must have been somewhat balanced if it held up until then."

Her eyes filled with tears. "I'm missing too many things to do this. The right potholders. My cooling racks. Cake stands. The measurements may have been the same, but these pans are deeper and heavier than I'm used to. I haven't reached for one thing that feels right. It's all different and awkward…"

Gideon stepped around the cake mass and opened the cabinet below the sink. He pulled a disposable cup out of a package and then filled it with water. Putting a firm hand on her shoulder, he guided her toward a stool and passed her the water. She seemed on the verge of hysteria, and he wanted to assure her. "Mattie Lane, you are strong enough to—"

"Ohhh," she growled, cutting him off. "Please don't treat me like I'm going to break from stress. I'm not that fragile, Gideon."

Her voice was filled with emotion, and pink tinged her cheeks. She'd been dealt a lot of blows in life, and he realized he'd always considered her fragile—a delicate, mysterious seedling in need of perfect soil, sun, and water.

She went to the sink, wet a washcloth, and began wiping splotches of cake and frosting from her dress, visibly shaking. But her emotional reaction didn't make her weak, and he'd been a fool to think it had.

She sighed, and a gentle, sad smile graced her beautiful face as a tear fell. "It might be my fault the shop caught fire."

"Whatever happened, it was an accident."

Her chin quivered. "I think I may have left our notebook on the wood stove."

Our notebook. The phrase worked its way into the recesses of his loneliness, bringing relief.

How strange life was. As she opened up to him the way she

had years ago, Gideon saw more than the hurt and disappointment pressing in on her. He saw strength. Wide and high and deep. And so very tender.

She ran her hands over her wet cheeks and sniffed. "Okay, enough of this." She pursed her lips. "Onward and upward." She rolled her eyes and gestured at the cake. "Or onward and downward, as the case may be."

He got a pan out of the sink to put the mounds of cake into, but Mattie Lane grabbed two forks and sat on the floor. She waved a fork over the highest area in the center. "None of this part touched the floor."

Blinking, he took a fork and sat.

She wrinkled her nose. "Remember our first cake?"

He chuckled. "We thought it was supposed to be an upside-down backside cake, right?"

The smile on her face spoke of friendship. "The Bundt cake that we thought was called a Bum cake." She laughed. "Mamm helped me bake it. After it cooled, we had the brilliant idea to make it the perfect Bum cake. I dumped it out of the pan onto a chair, and you sat on it."

He tugged at his pants as if airing them out. "It needed to be a lot cooler than it was when I sat on it. I remember that much."

Her laughter bounced off the walls of the empty home, refreshing his weary soul.

He pointed at her. "And again, I got in trouble, and your family thought you were adorable." He hadn't really gotten in trouble, but his grandmother did lecture him that at ten years old he should know to eat food, not sit on it.

She jabbed her fork into the cake. "Admit it, Gideon. You liked taking the blame, as long as it kept me out of trouble."

He didn't need to confess that, but he saw the truth of it more and more. If he'd seen her as the capable young woman she really was, would he have lied to her?

He took a bite of cake. "I remember the cake you made when we were teens. It was so hard that Beiler Construction used it as a cornerstone when we built a new house."

She laughed. "It wasn't that bad! Besides, you passed me the baking powder and said it was baking soda."

"Oh, ya, sure. Blame me." He swallowed a piece of cake, enjoying these few moments. Memories of them as children faded as ones of their courtship took over. "Remember when we came home all wet from our first canoe trip down the Susquehanna?"

Her eyes grew large, and she chortled. They'd gone down the river with a group of strangers, and a snake had dropped out of a tree onto an Englischer guy. The man panicked, tipping over the canoe. "We always were the talk of the community. What was it your grandmother used to call us?"

"Huck Finn and Becky Thatcher."

"Ah, right." Mattie lifted her chin to constrict her neck. "You kids remind me," she said, mimicking his grandmother's high-pitched, elderly voice, "of two peas in a pod. Life is just a blink, and you two sure know how to make it count."

After a hearty round of laughter at her imitation, quietness surrounded them, and her blue eyes smiled at him.

She stretched out her legs and leaned back against the cabinet. "It's good to see you laugh, Gideon. You've changed. Not so much in ways I can point my finger at, but it's there inside you. A hardness of some type that rarely gives way to the man I once knew. I guess losing Ashley took a lot out of you."

His heart palpitated, feeling as if weights were being lifted from it. "I'm so sorry, Mattie Lane."

She tilted her head, studying him. "Ya, I believe you are. We could wipe the slate clean now if you like."

"How so?"

"We can pretend you broke up with me the right way."

He tried to imagine being barely twenty-two again with the news he'd gotten and what he'd do differently this time. But he didn't know the answer.

She pointed her fork at him. "Regardless of how it happened, I'm actually glad I moved to Ohio to start my shop."

He stared at her, waiting for her to say she was also glad she met Sol.

She stood and washed her hands and face in the sink and then grabbed a towel.

"You seem to really like living there."

"Ya, I do. But I chose to start my business there for two reasons: it was far removed from you, and my parents peacefully accepted the change because I could live under the safety and affordability of James's roof. Not sure there's much calling me back now that the shop burned."

He propped his forearm on his knee, trying to sense her thoughts. Since she hadn't mentioned Sol, he wanted to believe that he didn't matter that much to her, but maybe he was seeing what he wanted to see. Even if it was true, Sol was better for her. Gideon had broken her heart once. If she came back to him and the cancer returned, he'd end up hurting her even worse.

Gideon stood. "Mattie Lane," he said softly, "if Sol's not the one, please don't settle."

"What?" She locked eyes with him, confusion evident.

"You didn't mention him as a reason to return."

"Oh." She got a large bowl out of the sink, knelt beside the mound of cake on the floor, and started tossing bits and pieces into it. "It's just that his job could be done anywhere, so we wouldn't have to live in Ohio."

"He builds pallets for a corporation, right?"

She glanced up. "How would you know that?"

Gideon couldn't stomach telling her another lie. "I asked your brother James about him once."

She raised her eyebrows and waited, letting him know that his answer was not sufficient.

He shrugged. "I needed to be sure you were seeing someone safe."

She returned to dumping cake in the pan, but a slight smile crossed her face. "I'm very safe with Sol. You don't need to worry about that." She stood and carried the bowl to the trash can. "I'm going to be here all night making fresh cakes. I'll need kerosene lanterns."

"I can get some at the dry goods store. You need anything else?"

"That should do it."

"How about a new cake stand?"

"No, I'm fine. I'll just scale back my fancy plans a bit this time." Her eyes met his. "Denki, Gideon."

Her thank-you seemed to hold a dozen messages—gratefulness that they'd patched up what they could between them and that he'd helped her release some of her frustrations over losing her shop. But it also seemed to carry a message of finality, as if they'd gone as far as they ever would in this relationship—two friends who'd go their separate ways all too soon.

Twelve

With a pastry bag in hand, Mattie stood in Beth and Jonah's finished home, working on their wedding cake. The pleasure of creating and decorating it bounced around inside her with as much energy as was displayed in the rest of the house. Voices echoed off the walls as people came in and out like travelers at a train station.

Lizzy and Omar had married last week, and their wedding cake had been lovely. She'd used dark beige fondant with light beige icing for their apricot-praline cake. The rope design she'd run along the sides and the flowers of the same color on top had accomplished the desired look.

Beth and Jonah had chosen the strawberries-and-cream vanilla cake with chocolate ganache and vanilla pastry-cream filling, so Mattie had used a white fondant with deep red flowers draping down the side.

But it was the cake she'd made for tonight's prewedding

dinner that pleased her most. Unlike the other cakes, she'd been able to work on this one with her Mamm, keeping the hours to a minimum and spread out over a week. She expected Beth and Jonah to get a kick out of how she'd decorated tonight's cake.

Gideon had come to the house one evening on an errand for his grandmother, and even seeing it in the early stages, he seemed awed by her imagination and skill.

Tomorrow was Beth and Jonah's big day. As excited as Mattie was to be a part of their wedding, she and Gideon had already spent too much time together. And neither would get away with disappearing during any part of the festivities. Jonah had chosen him to be the Amish equivalent of a best man, and she was Beth's equivalent of a maid of honor. By Amish tradition those positions had to be filled by unmarried people. Since all of Beth's and Jonah's siblings were married, that role fell to cousins and close friends.

She had to get away from this place as soon as possible.

Lizzy backed in the door, carrying armloads of folded white tablecloths. Another round of cold air surged inside. "The bride's table goes there." Lizzy directed the half-dozen men helpers as easily as she ran her store. They quickly set up lacquered wooden picnic tables and benches in the main living area, and Mattie helped Lizzy dust them until they virtually glowed in the light of the kerosene lanterns.

Several men entered, carrying stacks of folding chairs.

"Those need to be set up in the basement, leaving a center aisle for the couple to walk down," Lizzy ordered.

At Lizzy and Omar's wedding last week, Mattie had managed to avoid being around during the Choosing—a time late in the afternoon when single girls of the age to be courted lined up in a room, and the single men entered one at a time, from oldest to youngest, and chose a girl to pair up with for the rest of the festivities. She'd disappeared during that time, using the excuse that her Mamm and Daed were exhausted and she needed to take them home. Her Mamm told her that when Gideon attended weddings after Mattie left, he'd used that same trick, taking his grandmother home.

Had he not dated anyone since Ashley died? Since he'd joined the faith, he wouldn't have dated an Englischer women. And part of joining the faith was agreeing to seek a wife within the Amish community. She pushed those thoughts aside, demanding her mind to get off Gideon and what his life had been like the past three years. All she had to do was get through the wedding tomorrow and the cleanup the next day, and she could keep her distance from him until she boarded the train at midnight on Monday, which would put her in Ohio a full four days before Christmas Eve.

Mattie helped Lizzy spread the white linen cloths over the long rectangular tables set up in the main room. They lit kerosene floor lanterns as the evening grew darker, making the rooms much brighter.

"Hey, Lizzy," someone called from another part of the house. "Could you come here?"

"On my way."

Lizzy hurried off. Mattie easily tuned out the goings-on around her so she could remain focused on putting the final touches of frosting on the cake. She wished tuning out her thoughts about Gideon were as simple. She'd forgiven him for his misconduct, and now they got along just as well as they always had. Too well.

He'd been really helpful lately, designing and building cake stands to her specifications. He'd also built her a set of professional cooling racks that he said he'd ship to Ohio when the time came. He was the man she'd fallen in love with—giving and caring.

She couldn't remember the last time Sol had offered to help her with anything to do with her making cakes. But that's not who she and Sol were. They made a good couple because they worked well independently and then scheduled time together around their busyness. Lots of couples did that, probably most.

A loud thud resounded through the house, and she jumped, almost smearing the delicate green leaf she'd been working on. "You're supposed to be setting up tables and benches, not tearing the house down," Mattie said loudly, teasing whoever had dropped the piece of furniture.

"Sorry." A male voice echoed back at her.

Mattie switched pastry bags and added a tiny red flower to the side of the wedding cake.

Jonah walked in, carrying a bench. "You seen Lizzy?"

Mattie's aunt flew into the room before she could answer. "Where does this one go?"

"The second bedroom."

"Denki." Jonah nodded and kept going. Lizzy followed.

Beth came in the back door, juggling several large pots and pans that would be used to serve the wedding feast. "There's four inches of snow out there. It's gorgeous." Beth put the pots on the stove and moved to the counter to admire the cake. Again. "It's more lovely than I could've hoped for."

"It hasn't changed much since the last time you saw it."

"I know, but it looks prettier every time I swing through here." Beth rinsed her hands in the sink.

Lizzy came into the foyer on her way to the front door. "We're on schedule, Beth."

"You're amazing," Beth called after her. "That means we'll be done setting up for tomorrow in about five minutes, and everyone is going to Lizzy's to eat. You're going to join us, right?"

"Ya, but I need to do a few more things. I'll walk over as soon as I can."

"More? It's remarkable already."

"Denki. But I'll be the one who decides when I'm done," she teased. "Now, go away so I can finish."

Beth laughed. "Wow, it's a good thing I know you love me."

The racket in the house slowly died down until it became silent. Mattie moved to the kitchen window, watching large white flakes swirl against the dark sky. The shortest day of the year was fast approaching. She stepped onto the back porch. The night air smelled of Christmas.

"Mattie Lane."

Gideon's voice scattered her but also warmed her.

She turned. His gaze held hers, and she tried to lower her eyes.

"We ran out of seats, so Lizzy sent me after one of the benches. Jonah said to tell you it's perfect weather to hitch a horse to the sleigh, so we're doing that after dinner and taking turns going for rides."

Was he asking her to go for a sleigh ride with him? "I can't." She was desperate to keep her distance from him.

He nodded.

"But I could use a hand getting the cake to Lizzy's." She went inside to the wash house and took the celebration cake out of hiding.

Gideon studied it, nodding. "That's really something."

The large sheet cake had edible stencil cutouts and sculpturing that portrayed scenes from Beth and Jonah's story—Jonah in a shop, carving; Beth seeing the carving for the first time; and them writing to each other. Since Beth had thought she was writing to an elderly man at the time, Mattie put a few words on one of the tiny sheets of edible paper.

Dear old man ~

Then she'd made a happily-ever-after scene in which Jonah rescued Beth in a sleigh on a snowy Christmas Eve.

Mattie sighed. "What a love story they've had. And it's only the beginning."

It was a stark contrast to her and Gideon; they were nearing the end of their story, a final *the end.* She'd go to Ohio. He'd stay here. They'd barely catch a glimpse of each other after this trip, and it would likely be under different circumstances, since one of them might be married.

"So." Mattie set the celebration cake on the kitchen counter beside the wedding cake. "Did you come on foot or in a rig?"

"Can't carry a bench in a rig."

"True. After you deliver the bench, could you come back in a rig? The cake isn't so big I can't tote it, and I know Lizzy's is less than four hundred feet from here, but it's a little slippery out there, and I'd like to get this to her place without it landing upside down in the snow."

He chuckled. "I'll be back in a few."

Mattie went to the sink and washed her empty pastry bags and the multitude of tips, along with the rest of the dirty dishes from the day. While she was wiping down the countertops, someone knocked on the front door. She opened it to find Ashley's sister. Sympathy for the young woman tugged at her.

"Is Gideon here?" Sabrina didn't appear too happy, but she looked festive in her red coat.

"Not at the moment. But he'll be back shortly. Come in."

"Thanks." She stomped her snowy boots on the doormat, then came into the house.

"You do know he doesn't live here, right?"

"I know. But he's been here every time I've stopped by since he started working on this place." She peeled out of her coat, revealing decidedly non-Amish attire of stretchy, tight black pants and a hot pink sweater that accentuated every curve from her low neckline to the tops of her thighs. Mattie felt like a brown mouse next to her. She took off her gloves, stuffed them into her coat pockets, and stretched out her free hand. "I'm Sabrina."

"Mattie."

Something akin to shock passed through her eyes. "You're Mattie Lane?"

She took Sabrina's coat and hung it on one of the pegs by the front door. "Ya."

She fluffed out her short black hair. "I saw you here a few weeks ago, didn't I?"

"Ya, you did."

She smiled. "Ashley never liked that he broke up with you. She'd be pleased that the two of you are back together."

That was just odd. Why would Ashley disapprove of Gideon ending a relationship with another girl? "We're not back together. I'm going home to Ohio in a few days."

"Oh. Sorry."

"I'm sorry about your sister."

Her eyes clouded. "He told you?"

"Ya."

Sabrina sniffled and then gave a small smile. "Wow. This place has never smelled so good."

"That'd be the cakes I made today." Mattie led Sabrina to the kitchen.

Her mouth fell open when she saw the two cakes. "These are remarkable. Gideon told me you made cakes, but he never said you were this good."

Why would Gideon say anything at all about her? "Well, I've improved a lot." She took the almost dry pastry bag from the drainer and patted it with a towel. "He...talked to you about me?"

"Only all the time. It's one of the reasons I like him so much. He's got a really good heart. Not many out there like him." Sabrina's eyes widened. "Sorry. I guess it's out of line to say that about an old boyfriend."

"I've met someone else."

"Ashley warned him you would. She told him to be honest with you."

Honest? Feeling as if she was missing entire segments of this conversation, she wanted to ask Sabrina to clarify what she meant. "She sounds like a good person."

"She was. She believed with all her heart that she and Gideon would both beat that awful disease. But there's no predicting who will beat it." The girl's voice grew thick.

Mattie's breath caught in her throat, and her mind ground to a halt. *Both?* Gideon had it too? Suddenly it dawned on her that she'd never once asked Gideon how he met Ashley.

Sabrina returned her attention to the wedding cake. "Did you go to school to learn how to do this? Or does it come naturally to you?"

Her words garbled in Mattie's brain, and she couldn't respond. Everything around her seemed to be happening in slow motion, as if she were in a dream. *Leukemia?*

Gideon walked inside. He stopped short when he saw Sabrina. "Hey there. What are you doing here?"

"I have to leave on my trip tomorrow, and I wanted to see you first."

He shot a glance at Mattie. Then he led Sabrina to the front door, helped her into her coat, and took her arm as they went outside.

Mattie inhaled a halting breath. She poured herself a glass of water, trembling as she gulped it down.

He had cancer. Missing bits and pieces to understanding Gideon dangled just out of reach. She could see the scraps now, but they made little sense.

Reeling in shock, she tried to review the events of three years ago, overlaying what she'd perceived had happened with this new perspective.

What had he done?

Thirteen

*G*ideon walked Sabrina to her car. No stars were visible, and the air seemed pitch black as white snowflakes fell all around them.

Sabrina opened her trunk and passed him a present. "You can't open that until Christmas, but since I won't be in town to deliver it then, I'm going to have to trust you."

He bounced the package up and down. "At least I know it's not another five pounds of fudge."

She laughed. "Ashley made me promise you'd always get a Christmas present. She thought it'd help remove some of the sting of loneliness that swallows people in your position."

She was right. Battling cancer had an unbearable isolation to it. Not wanting to get sucked down that hole, he teased, "What, you mean a man without a girlfriend?"

"No, silly. Although I just met your Mattie Lane."

"She's not mine, not anymore."

"Maybe it's not too late."

"It was too late years ago."

"There's always a chance for Christmas magic. You tell me that every year."

"Not in this case. Mattie's going to Ohio to build a life with her guy, and I'm staying here."

"I'm sorry."

Her words summed up his own feelings. He'd always love Mattie.

He held up the package. "Thanks for bringing this. Now go. Have enough fun in Europe for both of us."

"Merry Christmas, Gideon." She hugged him before hopping into her car. He waved as Sabrina pulled out of the driveway.

Something grabbed his arm and jerked him. When he turned, Mattie's features were taut, and her eyes held disbelief as frigid winds thrashed at her dress and apron. "What have you done?"

His thoughts splintered into a dozen directions, trying to figure out what she was referring to. "About what?"

"How could you?" Her muted shriek came from deep within.

He swallowed hard, fearing Sabrina had revealed his secret.

And he also had a distant, uncontrollable hope that she had.

He took Mattie's arm to keep her from falling on the slick ground. "Let's go inside."

She pulled away, slapping at his arms through his thick coat. "Stop babying me," she hissed.

He held up his hands and backed away. "Okay."

She jerked a breath into her lungs. "I want you to tell me the truth. Can you do that?"

"If I do, it'll open doors to things we've both locked away. Just let it be."

"I want answers, Gideon." She balled her hands into fists. "Truthful ones!"

He nodded. "Okay, I promise, nothing but complete honesty."

She glanced heavenward, disgust and hurt written in her eyes. After a few moments she focused on him, looking a little more in control of her emotions. "What did you do three years ago?"

He took off his coat and put it around her shoulders. She stared at him without moving. He tugged on the collar of it. The temptation to say, "I've loved you for a lifetime, Mattie Lane," was almost too strong to conquer. Instead, he said, "After months of feeling bad and going to doctors who were no help, I…was diagnosed with leukemia."

Horror filled her features. "Gideon." Her whisper held deep

pity, and he was reminded of another reason he'd lied to her. He didn't want her to stay by his side out of pity. "Are you still sick?"

He shook his head. "No, not right now."

Relief flickered in her eyes for a moment.

"I'd planned on telling you about my illness after the holidays. But then Ashley came to me with devastating news." He steadied his voice as best he could. "She was cancer free one day and facing a grueling battle the next. What hope did I have…what life could I offer you? You arrived at my place minutes after she told me her latest diagnosis. Knowing my cancer had gone from a bad stage to a worse one, I…did what I thought would be best for you in the long run."

Her face contorted with confusion. "Did you love me?"

"With every breath I've ever drawn."

"Then why, Gideon?" She sounded close to hysteria.

"Imagine we were in a buggy traveling together and an eighteen-wheeler was gunning for me. All I could think of was getting you out, Mattie. Getting you to safety."

"Do you have any idea what you did to me?" she screamed, shaking her fists in the air.

"Ya. I spared you. I was in isolation for nearly nine months after a bone marrow transplant. I came so close to dying time and again and was too sick to hold up my head; I couldn't work. The treatments cost an incredible amount of money. Every penny I'd saved for our life together is gone. A government program had to take over covering the medical costs. I was powerless to do anything worthwhile...except that I'd let you go before it got that bad." He drew a breath, trying to close the dam of pain before they both drowned in it. "You were brokenhearted when your mother was diagnosed with lupus. I couldn't bear to put you through all that again with me. I didn't want you trapped in a life you'd seek rescue from."

"Rescue? Do you think I wanted to be saved from Mamm's illness?" She held her hands open, thrusting them palms up as she spoke. "What? Do you think I'd have chosen to have a different Mamm just so I wouldn't have to go through that hardship?"

"No, of course not. But your Mamm's health has always been fragile, and you've had a heavy weight on you since you were little, long before she got lupus."

"Open your eyes, Gideon Beiler." She waved a finger in his face. "Sure, I've grieved for Mamm, but because of her fragility, I learned how to embrace each day with her as if it might be our last. I learned how to love and give without allowing her illness to pull me under."

"But it did take its toll, day after day, year in and year out."

"Tears and sleepless nights are not signs of weakness. Jesus wept a few times in His life, and He was awake a lot while others slept. Does that mean He was too weak to cope? Or was He showing the depth and power of His compassion?"

Gideon wished he could make her see his point, but no counterargument came to him.

Mattie ducked her head, fighting tears. "It's impressive that you had the strength to shut me out and go through that journey on your own, but you needed to have found the strength to let me in." She lifted her chin. "Look at who I am. I spend months planning and preparing cakes that are marred with the first slice and devoured in minutes." She drew a shaky breath. "But having something that I've worked on taken apart doesn't make me give up. It's the thrill of creating it and the joy it brings to others and the memories it gives that matter. That's who I am. I wouldn't have given up on you out of fear of what the future might bring. I would have done my best to make our lives a beautiful creation while enjoying whatever time we had."

He heard sleigh bells in the distance. Someone was coming toward them. This conversation would end soon, and he wasn't sure when they'd have another opportunity to speak so openly.

She stepped close and tugged on his shirt. "But I have no idea who you are. I haven't for a really long time." She took his coat off her shoulders and held it out to him. "I'm sorry about everything you've been through. But in your effort to protect me, you killed the one person who mattered the most to me—you."

"Hello." Jonah brought the sleigh to a stop a few feet away from them.

Beth clapped her gloved hands. "You two have taken too long to come to Lizzy's, and we've come to get you."

"Wait, I'll be right back." Mattie disappeared into the house and moments later came out wearing her own coat and carrying the celebration cake.

"What's that?" Beth asked.

Mattie passed it to her. "It's a gift for you and your guests to enjoy tonight. But I'd like to go home. Would you mind dropping me off?"

"Of course not," Jonah said.

"I can't really see all the detail right now," Beth said, examining the cake in the dark, "but I can tell it's exquisite."

"Mattie Lane," Gideon whispered, "don't go like this."

She ignored him.

Beth lifted a blanket. "Kumm. We'll drop the cake off at Lizzy's and be on our way."

Jonah helped Mattie into the sleigh. "Gideon, will you take Mattie's horse and rig home so she'll have it for the morning?"

"Ya." He stood alone as they drove off, knowing that the only thing more devastating than having a serious illness was the destruction wrought while trying to cover it up.

Fourteen

Mattie's head throbbed as she sat at the bride-and-groom table next to Gideon, trying to eat. Six hours ago in the basement filled with loved ones seated on folding chairs, Jonah had walked Beth down the aisle in this house—their home. Beth wore a crisp burgundy wine cape dress with a sheer white cape and apron in place of the usual black one. Mattie had on the exact same outfit, as did the other girls in the bridal party.

Traditionally, Amish couples got married in the home of the bride's parents or an uncle, so today was very unusual—like Beth and Jonah themselves.

Beth sat across from Jonah, and Gideon sat between Beth and Mattie. The placement of who sat where was a tradition that had probably begun hundreds of years ago, possibly longer. But Mattie couldn't take much more of being paired with Gideon.

Her thoughts were a jumbled mess. The idea of Gideon

going through treatment without her support tormented her. She felt as if he'd just received the diagnosis, and the realization that he'd shut her out while trying to protect her made everything worse.

What was she supposed to think...or feel? He'd broken her heart, and, unknowingly, she'd been furious with him while he spent two years battling for his life.

Beth leaned behind Gideon, who was chatting with Jonah, and caught Mattie's attention. "Gideon will lead the first round of songs, so be sure to tell him some of your favorites."

Mattie did her best to keep a smile pasted on for Beth's benefit, hoping not to dampen her cousin's celebration. "I think I'll choose some sad, pitiful dirges," she teased, "to match your mood today."

Beth laughed.

When Mattie sat forward, her eye caught Gideon's, and it was all she could do to keep from bursting into tears. He'd betrayed her—both of them, really. When the main part of the meal was over, a multitude of women removed dirty tableware. Lizzy cut the cake and dished it onto dessert plates, and Beth's sisters-in-law and aunts served everyone. Mattie enjoyed the *ooh*s over Beth and Jonah's wedding cake and received compliments galore once people took a bite of it. Whatever else Gideon had destroyed or stolen, he hadn't ruined the part of her that was a cake maker and decorator.

A distant, fuzzy thought tried to enter her consciousness, and she turned to Gideon as if studying him would bring clarity. He said he'd asked her brother James about Sol, but when? There was no way Gideon had talked to James on her phone at the store. And until her shop burned, James never went to the Kings' store to use their phone. Had Gideon spent his limited strength and money to come to Ohio to check on her?

He turned to face her, and she knew he had. How many times had he come to Berlin in the last three years?

"Just think about our canoe ride down the Susquehanna... and the wild dance that man performed before he tipped us over," Gideon whispered.

She allowed a weak smile to surface. Is that what got him through—thinking about their good times?

The endless questions were on her last nerve, and she wished they'd stop.

In a few minutes she could leave this spot and maybe be able to breathe again. By tradition, when the meal ended, close family would wash dishes and clean up while the bride and groom, their friends, and the other guests visited or freshened up. In an hour or so, everyone would reconvene for songs and rounds of snacks. She scanned the room, looking for her escape.

Mamm was going into a spare bedroom with a stack of wrapped gifts. That'd be a quiet, out-of-the-way place to hide for a bit. When Beth and Jonah got up to mingle, Mattie knew she could disappear without being missed. She wound her way through the crowd, but before she got to the closed door of the bedroom, her Mamm opened it and stepped out.

Mamm grinned, shutting the door behind her. "Sorry, Mattie, this room is off-limits to anyone trying to take a peek at the gifts."

Mattie fought the desire to shrink into her mom's arms and weep.

Mamm's smile faded into concern. "Mattie, sweetheart." She cupped her face with her soft hands. "I thought you'd feel better today."

Tears welled in Mattie's eyes, and Mamm took her by the hand, led her into the room, and locked the door behind them. "You came home early last night and went straight to bed. And now you're sad. What's wrong?"

Mattie wiped her tears. "Gideon didn't break up with me because of someone else. He lied about her, about a lot of things."

Mamm stared wide-eyed. "Are you still in love with him?"

Mattie couldn't answer her. She went into the half bath and rinsed her face, the cool water easing the burning in her eyes. "I might have thought I was yesterday, but how can I be?" She buried her face in a towel, trying to get control. She took a breath. "I don't know who he is."

"I was disappointed in him when he broke up with you. Truth of the matter is, I was really angry that he'd hurt you." Mamm tightened her hands into fists and shook them before she smiled. "And if I'd seen him out and about, I might've scolded him, but he left Apple Ridge about the same time you did. During the first two years, I heard he returned for two or three days around Christmas. Then about a year ago, he returned for good, and I was at Verna's when he came in. He didn't look anything like the man who'd left here. But I talked with him for a bit. I don't remember what it was about, but I saw…" She tapped the center of her chest. "I saw with the same part of me that sees God, and I knew right then that whatever took place between you two, he's the same man he's always been—patient, kind, and trustworthy."

Mattie scoffed. "I'm pretty confident he's not trustworthy, but I think…" She twisted the hand towel into a thick rope and moved from the tiny bathroom to the edge of the bed. "I *know* he still loves me. He's never stopped loving me."

"But you care for Sol now."

"At least he's not a liar. Gideon deceived me when he broke up with me. He was sick, Mamm, and he didn't want me to know."

"Sick?" she whispered. "Oh." A faraway look entered her eyes. "Now it all makes sense, doesn't it?"

"Don't you see? His confession, which he made only because he was cornered with the truth, makes him a fraud and a hypocrite."

"Oh, Mattie, sweetheart." Mamm's face crumpled, sadness and understanding shadowing her smile. She sat beside her. "If I could have spared you, my little sweet-sixteen girl, and your Daed from having to know about and cope with my illness, I would have."

"What? No you wouldn't."

"Ya, I would've. And even though your brothers were married with homes of their own, I'd have spared them the heartache too if I'd known how. It may be the one dream shared by everyone struck with illness. If we could find a way, we'd keep our loved ones from shouldering the strain and hurt, from having their quality of life jerked away from them."

Unable to accept what her mother had said, Mattie went to the window. Last night's fresh layer of snow was marred and ugly because of people shoveling it out of the way, driving rigs across it, or walking through it. She felt like that snow looked. But life caused people to have to move about, and that meant mucking up the once-pristine landscape.

Mamm came to her side and put her arm around Mattie's waist. "I always thought that his wanting to see other girls was a lie. I've asked your brothers and their children who are your age, and no one ever saw him with another girl. They say he's never gone to singings…except the Christmas ones. Even then, he came and left by himself."

She'd loved their first date, when he took her to the Christmas singing, so much that she'd made him promise he'd always go until they were married. And it sounded as if he'd kept that promise, even when she wasn't there to see it.

Mattie closed her eyes. "Why didn't anyone tell me?"

"Because it wasn't our place. All we had was our speculation, and you assured me that you didn't want to talk to Gideon about anything, that you just wanted to move to Berlin. So we let you. It was a year later when we saw him looking so poorly and attending a singing by himself. By that time your new business was taking off, and you were starting to see Sol, and we thought you were happy."

Her self-righteous attitude melted. "What am I supposed to do? I'm with Sol."

"Then explain that to Gideon. He set you free to do just that, didn't he?"

"I didn't want to be set free."

Mamm lifted Mattie's chin and looked into her eyes. "Mattie, do you love Sol?"

She wished Mamm hadn't asked that. "I care for him a lot. But I'm not ready to marry him tomorrow."

"Next year then?"

She shrugged. "Maybe."

"It's okay to hate the sin of lying, but have mercy on the man who loves you more than himself."

She blinked her eyes, trying not to cry. "I can't hurt Sol."

"If you love him, don't let anything stop you from marrying him. But if you marry him for the wrong reasons, you *will* hurt him for years and years. And you'll hurt yourself and Gideon too." Mamm took her hand. "Now, kumm. I need to finish bringing presents in here, and you need to be fellowshipping with Beth and Jonah's guests. Everyone here is buzzing about the cakes you made for these weddings."

Her Mamm was so proud of her, but if she could see how selfishly her daughter acted at times, it'd wound her. When Mattie had moved to Ohio, she'd wasted no time starting to date others. What she should've done was take a little time to figure out why Gideon suddenly wanted to be free of her. But no, not her. She was too proud and too busy reorganizing her dreams to waste any time on him.

Halfway down the hallway Mattie tugged on Mamm's hand, and she stopped. Mattie hugged her. "Denki."

"Gern gschehne."

As they left the hallway, Mattie saw Gideon across the room, standing near a window, talking with Aden Zook. In spite of his sin, his heart had been in the right place. And she did know who he was.

He glanced up, and a timid smile touched his lips.

"Mamm, I need to see Gideon."

"Sure, honey. You go on."

Mattie walked toward him. After excusing himself to Aden, Gideon met her halfway.

"I understand now."

Surprise crossed his face. "You do?"

"Ya. But I still have to go back to Ohio next week."

The look in his eyes intensified. "That's what I've wanted all along, Mattie Lane."

Sadness held on so tight she felt numb. "Is that really all, for me to know the truth and return to Sol?"

His face showed no emotion that she recognized. "Pretty much, ya."

Raising her eyebrows, she waited.

"It's silly, but I thought it'd be nice if we had one day together without anger or grief, just one day to be who we used to be."

"That would've been nice." But one day alone with Gideon without anger or grief would most certainly undo her. She slid her hand into his. "You stay well. You hear me?"

He squeezed her fingers tenderly. "Anything for you, Mattie Lane."

Fifteen

Something woke Gideon, and he rolled over, opening his eyes. The room was dark, and he wondered what time it was. Peace stirred, moving about in him like a construction team laying the foundation for a new home. Mattie knew everything and had forgiven him. That alone would sustain him after she left.

Something thudded against his window. He rose, slipped into his pants, and went to look out. Remnants of a snowball slid down the glass. He opened the window, and below, bathed in silvery moonlight and standing in several inches of new snow, Mattie gazed up at him. A horse stood behind her with Beth and Jonah's sleigh attached to it.

"Mattie Lane, what are you doing?"

She lobbed a snowball straight up into the air and backed away when it almost landed on her. It dropped inches in front of Jessie Bell, and the horse neighed, shaking her head. Mattie bit her bottom lip, smiling up at him like it was Christmas. "One day, Gideon Beiler. You asked for it, and you've got it. We have from now until I leave at eleven tonight. That's about nineteen hours to wreak some havoc as we travel down Mattie's lane."

He could hardly believe his ears. Or his eyes.

She pulled a rolled-up piece of paper out of her pocket. "I spent most the night working on this list." She held the top of it, and it unrolled from her head to the ground. "Number one: Go for a sleigh ride." She jingled the bells dangling on the horse's back. "Number two: Go tobogganing." She pointed at a long sled inside the sleigh. "Number three: Return here, and *you* fix us breakfast. Number four: Hire a driver and go to Harrisburg to watch the Susquehanna." She held up a pair of binoculars. "And I do mean *watch*. Not fall into it. Number five: Have lunch at the Fire House Restaurant before taking a tour of the historic district and visiting the State Museum of Pennsylvania. Number six: Go ice-skating on Miller's pond." She lowered the list. "Hey, do you still have my ice skates?"

"I'm wearing them right now."

She rolled her eyes. "Now, we're going to skate on Miller's pond if it's solid enough. If it's not, only you will go skating while I time how long it takes before the ice cracks and you have a cold swim."

"Thanks, Mattie."

She giggled and propped one hand on her waist and motioned impatiently with the other. "Well, hurry up. Nineteen hours isn't much time."

He dressed, and while hurrying down the steps, he put on his coat, scarf, and hat.

He opened the door, and she flung a snowball at him. He bent to scoop up a handful of snow, and when he stood, she was hiding behind the horse.

"No fair, Mattie Lane."

"All is fair inside the magical, mystical land known as Mattie Lane. How do you not know that by now?"

Mattie squeezed the pastry bag, draping thin loops of gold icing onto the Christmas cake. Her brother's home smelled of the holiday feast they'd have for dinner this evening, featuring turkey and stuffing, black-eyed peas, sweet potato pie, and green beans.

Her niece had her own pastry tube. Esther hummed and chatted while squirting mounds of icing onto a batch of cookies. The little girl had not moved from her kneeling position on a kitchen chair for nearly an hour. "Mattie Cakes, do you make your own birthday cake every year?"

Mattie tried to focus her mind, which was still suspended in a fog somewhere between Berlin, Ohio, and Apple Ridge, Pennsylvania. She'd hoped that going through her usual Christmas Eve traditions would lift the grief and confusion, perhaps scrub away some of the desire for Gideon, but that hadn't happened yet. "Ya, I do, sweetie."

James marched into the house, carrying a load of wood, and stomped snow off his boots. "Well, there are two of my favorite girls." He dumped the logs into the bin next to the open hearth. "Where are your big brothers and sisters, Esther?"

She put her index finger on her lips. "They're in their rooms with the doors locked, wrapping presents."

Mattie's eyes met her brother's, and they chuckled. Why did Esther act like the location of her older siblings was a secret?

Dorothy walked into the kitchen, carrying her youngest one on her hip.

James went to his wife, and they spoke quietly for a moment before sharing a long, lingering kiss. Esther glanced up, smiled at her parents' show of affection, then returned her attention to her cookie.

James walked to the edge of the table, amusement on his face. He lifted one of Esther's gooey cookies. "This much icing gives new meaning to the name *sugar cookies.*"

Esther glowed. "You like it, Daed?"

"These will be my all-time favorites." He set it down. "But not until after we eat our dinner."

Dorothy placed an empty mug in the sink. "Esther, have you made your bed?"

"I'm helping Mattie Cakes."

Dorothy looked to Mattie with a raised brow.

Ever since she'd returned from Pennsylvania, the only way Mattie had found any Christmas cheer was through her niece's innocent excitement. "It's true. She's telling me right where all the dots and curlicues need to go."

"And she helped me put my very own cake in the oven." Esther bobbed her little head up and down. "I get to decorate it after it's cool."

Dorothy flashed Mattie a look that was somewhere between gratitude and *you've got to be kidding me.*

James scooped his daughter off the chair. "We're going to have to rename you Mattie Cakes Two." He tapped her nose with his forefinger, making Esther giggle with delight.

Dorothy pulled a clean burp cloth out of a drawer. "But all bakers have to make their own beds and straighten their rooms, even on Christmas Eve."

Esther's eyes grew wide. "Is that true, Mattie Cakes?"

Mattie leaned in and kissed the top of her niece's head. "If your Mamm said so, it must be."

Esther hopped down from her father's arms and ran upstairs.

Mattie set the pastry bag with gold icing aside and picked up the one with red icing. "You know, she was in my attic room at the shop several times, and my bed was rarely made up."

Humor danced in Dorothy's eyes. "You don't want to know my response to that, do you?"

James plopped into a chair at the kitchen table. "Go ahead. She can take it."

Dorothy gave a sheepish grin. "I know this isn't true. It's just the first thing I thought when you said you didn't always make your bed."

"Well, out with it."

"I'd tell Esther, 'And you see what happened to her shop, don't you?'"

James laughed, then stopped short, mocking a guilty look for being amused.

Mattie couldn't help but chuckle. "You have a morbid sense of humor, Dorothy Eash."

"I do, don't I?" She sat beside her husband and put her youngest in the nursing position under a fold of her cape bodice. "Will Sol be here in time for our noon meal?"

Mattie glanced at the clock. Eleven fifteen, and she already thought the day would never end. "Today is the one day of the year I *can* expect him to come see me. He went hunting this morning, of course, so he might be a little late. But I bet he's here before we're finished eating so we can go early to the Christmas singing tonight."

The mirth faded from James's face. He pressed his index finger onto a crumb on the table. "You don't seem at all disappointed that he went hunting on your birthday or that he goes on more hunts than Daniel Boone."

Mattie squirted red frosting on the cake. "He does his thing, and I do mine. What's wrong with that?"

"Nothing," James said. He glanced at his wife. "Dorothy and I just want to be sure you're thinking clearly. Every brother and sister-in-law you have has been praying for you every day for years...especially since you and Gideon broke up."

Mattie pushed the cake away, her smidgen of a lighthearted mood gone. "I appreciate your prayers, but I don't need your advice or your meddling."

"Okay." James angled his head, catching her eye. "Just answer one question, and I'll never bring up this topic again."

She scowled at him. "Then by all means, ask it."

"What draws you to Sol?"

Frustration burned like hot coals in Mattie. "He's a good man who will never break my heart."

"I agree." Dorothy folded the burp cloth with one hand

while holding her baby. "It's impossible for him to break what he can't touch."

Dorothy's words left Mattie weak. She sank into the chair beside her sister-in-law, grief surrounding her as if she were buried in a snowbank. She could have a comfortable life with Sol. It would be void of passion and gusto, but it would be a long, smooth road.

The doorbell rang. Mattie looked through the kitchen window and saw a white truck. "Does FedEx deliver on Christmas Eve?"

James glanced outside. "I guess so."

Mattie hurried out of the room, glad to get away from the prying questions. She opened the door and found a small package on the doorstep. "Merry Christmas," she called to the man in the navy and purple uniform.

He waved while hurrying back to his truck. "Merry Christmas."

She picked up the box. The package was addressed to her. Eager for something to lift her spirits, she took it into the kitchen.

"Who's it from?" Dorothy asked.

"It doesn't say." Mattie got a knife from a drawer and slid it across the packing tape. Inside a layer of plastic bubble wrap, she saw a book. She pulled it out of the layers of protection.

A hand-drawn image of herself with a pastry bag in hand, decorating a four-tier wedding cake, graced the cover. Chills skittered up her spine. In the bottom left corner of the picture, the name Aden appeared in tiny letters.

She dropped into a chair and opened the book. The inside front flap had *Mattie Cakes Portfolio* scrawled on it. She gingerly turned the pages. Aden had meticulously drawn numerous cakes with familiar designs, using colored pencils to give each area the correct shade. At the bottom of every page, he'd written the name of the cake design and where the idea came from, as well as the year she first made it.

Her heart filled with emotions too big for her chest, like the Grinch's had in that kids' movie she'd seen years ago while baby-sitting. "Look at this."

James and Dorothy moved behind her, looking over her shoulder.

"How could Aden know all this? When I lived with Mamm and Daed, he came over a few times and made sketches of various stages of my work. But he never saw all these."

"Maybe he remembers them from your old scrapbook," Dorothy suggested.

She turned another page. "This is unbelievable. That man has more talent than I realized." She flipped to the next page, and her heart nearly stopped. "I made that cake in September.

There's no way Aden could have seen it." She looked up at James and Dorothy. "You're the only ones who could've told him about it."

"Wasn't me," James said. "I don't remember ever seeing that one."

Dorothy brought her infant out from the flap of her cape. "I need to put this little guy down for his nap."

"Dorothy, wait." Mattie stood. "You know something."

She looked to her husband as if asking to be rescued, but James just shrugged. Her face contorted into an apology. "That must be Gideon's doing."

Mattie's heart skipped. "But a few cakes I made last year are included, up to a few months before the shop burned. How would he know what to tell Aden to draw?"

Dorothy juggled her sleeping baby on her shoulder. "He, uh…used to come by here sometimes."

Mattie shot a glare at her. "I figured that out before I returned here, but I never saw him."

James stroked his beard. "He didn't want to upset you. He always stopped by while you were gone and asked how you were doing. If you left your book here, he'd take a peek at it. He'd do it casual-like, as if he was just curious, but we knew the truth."

And so did Mattie—Gideon loved her more than she'd ever hoped for. "Why didn't you tell me?"

James went to the stove and poured a cup of coffee. "You'd been here about a year when he made his first visit. It only took a glance at him to know he was as weak as a kitten. We never talked about it, but when I saw him so sick, I finally understood why he broke up with you." He took a sip of the hot, black liquid. "You were seeing Sol by then. Mattie Cakes was growing by leaps and bounds. And I respected what he was trying to do."

"We just want you to find the right man," Dorothy said. "If that's Sol, we're happy for you. He's a nice guy. We don't care for him the way we do Gideon, but we'd be honored to have him as a brother-in-law…if…"

"If what?"

James set his cup down hard. "If you haven't chosen him merely because he's a great guy who is incapable of breaking your heart."

With her heart pounding so hard she thought it might explode, Mattie looked through the book again. The fog that'd been so thick for more than a week began to lift. As hard as she'd tried to love someone else, her heart still belonged to Gideon.

But it was too late now.

"Knock, knock," Sol called as he came in the front door.

And she knew what had to be done. "Excuse me." Mattie went into the living room. "You're back earlier than I expected."

"I know. My watch stopped, and I wasn't sure of the time, so I came on back. It wouldn't do to make you angry on the one day we both know belongs under your rules."

"My rules?" she whispered. Was that all that motivated him to be here for the family Christmas Eve meal and her birthday?

She wondered if he remembered their first date. Or the first cake she'd made him. He probably didn't think such things mattered. And he'd be right. It didn't make any difference, because she wasn't in this relationship to be honored or loved. She just wanted companionship and convenience. Someone to spend a little time with when they finally looked up from the things they were passionate about—cake making and hunting. A man to tell others she was seeing while she kept her heart a safe distance from him. He didn't even know how to search for it. And she didn't blame him.

But Sol deserved to find someone who loved him the way she loved Gideon. Her Mamm was right—if she stayed for the wrong reasons, she'd hurt Sol, Gideon, and herself.

She picked up his coat off the couch and hung it on a peg. "Sol, could you sit with me for a few minutes?"

He removed his camouflage-colored toboggan. "Sure." He sat on the couch. "This doesn't sound good, so get to the point. Aim for the target and shoot."

She tried to focus all her thoughts and emotions into one

sentence that would make sense. "I'd rather have one day of giving love and being truly loved than a lifetime of convenient and comfortable."

He raked his hands through his unwashed hair. "Gideon."

"I'm sorry."

"I knew when I came to the hospital and saw him holding your hand that it'd be easy for him to win you back."

"And you cared enough to come to Pennsylvania to check on me."

"That should count for something."

"It does."

"But not enough?" He searched her eyes, looking for answers.

"I'm sorry," she repeated, feeling as if she needed to say it a thousand more times.

He sighed. "I've learned a lot from being with you. Even figured out how to talk to girls." He gave a slight chuckle. "Maybe now I can go to singings on my own and carry on a real conversation."

She touched his hand. "If you do, I'm sure you'll find the right girl for you."

"It won't be Katie King." He shuddered, and they both laughed. "If it doesn't work out with Gideon, you know where to find me."

"Ya." She smiled. "In a tree stand with a bow, gun, or muzzleloader." She pressed her apron with her hand. "Can you forgive me?"

He stood. "Maybe next week." His lopsided smile let her know he'd be fine without her. He grabbed his coat and went toward the door.

"You could stay and eat with us."

"I'm not hungry. Tell your family Merry Christmas for me." He gazed into her eyes. "And be happy, Mattie."

"Denki." She closed the door behind him, praying he'd find the right woman. Within minutes peace for him removed her concern, and her thoughts turned to Gideon.

Sixteen

The cold night air didn't stir, and the stars shone brightly in the clear sky as Gideon walked from his rig toward the Stoltzfuses' barn. The lyrics from "Silent Night" reverberated around him. It was the one night of the year that they sang some of the songs in English.

The promise he'd made to Mattie Lane was only half the reason he came to the singings every Christmas Eve. The other half was his hope that she'd return to him.

But it was time to let go. She knew everything she needed to, and she'd chosen Sol. On the one hand, that was what he wanted for her. On the other, he longed to spend whatever time he had left on this planet by her side.

He'd considered not coming to this singing, but he needed a way of saying a final good-bye to the hopes and dreams of sharing a life with Mattie Lane.

He opened the small door inside the huge sliding door and

walked into the barn. Much as they did in church, the females sat on benches on one side, males on the other. This time they were facing each other, and he took a seat on a bench toward the back.

Omar, who came to every singing as part of his responsibilities as bishop, brought him an *Ausbund,* an Amish book of songs written in German. He put one hand on Gideon's shoulder and squeezed.

Everyone now knew about his battle with leukemia. After his secret was divulged to Mattie, he had no reason to keep living a lie. He confessed his sin to the congregation, and Omar, as the church's authority figure, forgave him. Gideon had to show signs of repentance, and Omar's edict said he must be the lead carpenter on a new mission home. Every two to three years, the Amish community collected money and worked together to build a place for a homeless non-Amish family. These mission homes were a way of helping the poor and building good relations with Englischers.

Gideon had intended to help build the house anyway, and Omar knew it. Making him the lead carpenter was an honor— one that would help put the name of Beiler Construction in the news. Omar knew that too.

Gideon closed his eyes, grateful to finally be forgiven for the lie he'd told. Never again would he be so foolish as to think he could control anyone or anything through false words. He'd speak truth always and pray for God's strength over those who might struggle under the weight of the truth.

He joined in on the chorus.

"Silent night, holy night. All is calm…"

The girls stopped singing and stared at the back of the barn, whispering. Some of the guys stopped too, turning to see what had their attention. Gideon looked behind him.

Mattie Lane.

She smiled warmly, and he knew…she'd come back to him. He went toward her, and she opened her arms. He wrapped her in a tight embrace. Tears stung his eyes, and he couldn't find his voice.

She backed away, caressing his face with her hands. "Mackenzie brought me in exchange for me promising that I'd tell you the full truth."

"You can tell me anything."

"I love you, Gideon Beiler."

He pulled her close, not caring about the unspoken rules of proper behavior. Unable to find his voice, he pressed his lips against hers. He still had no idea how much time he had left— maybe a lifetime.

But whatever God gave them, it was enough.

3-Layer Strawberries-and-Cream Cake

2 cups sugar

1 small package strawberry gelatin

1 cup butter, softened

4 eggs

2$\frac{3}{4}$ cups cake flour

2$\frac{1}{2}$ teaspoons baking powder

1 cup milk

1 teaspoon vanilla

$\frac{1}{2}$ cup strawberries, puréed

Preheat oven to 350°. Grease and flour three 9-inch, round cake pans. In a large mixing bowl, beat sugar, gelatin, and butter until fluffy. Add eggs one at a time, beating after each. Mix the flour and baking powder together, and add to the sugar mixture in two parts, alternating with the milk and beating after each addition. Fold in vanilla and puréed strawberries. Divide equally into the three cake pans.

Bake for 25 minutes. Cool for 10 minutes in the pans, then remove from the pans and cool completely.

Filling:

1$\frac{1}{2}$ cups heavy whipping cream

2 tablespoons sugar

$^1/_2$ teaspoon vanilla

$1^1/_2$ cups fresh strawberries, sliced

Beat the whipping cream, sugar, and vanilla until stiff. Cover the bottom and middle cake layer each with $^1/_3$ of the whipped cream and $^3/_4$ cup sliced strawberries. Set aside remaining whipped cream.

Frosting:

$^1/_2$ cup butter, softened

8-ounce package cream cheese, softened

4 cups powdered sugar

2 teaspoons vanilla

$1^1/_2$ cup fresh strawberries, halved or quartered

Beat the butter, cream cheese, powdered sugar, and vanilla until creamy. Spread frosting around the sides of the cake. Make a pretty piping of frosting along the top edge of the cake. Gently spread remaining whipped cream on cake top. Decorate top with strawberries.

Orange Coconut Cake

1$\frac{1}{2}$ sticks unsalted butter, at room temperature

1$\frac{1}{4}$ cups sugar

4 eggs, at room temperature; separate yolks and whites

2 cups cake flour

2 teaspoons baking powder

$\frac{1}{4}$ teaspoon salt

$\frac{1}{2}$ cup buttermilk or coconut milk

1 teaspoon coconut extract

1 teaspoon grated lemon zest

Preheat oven to 350°. Grease and flour two 9-inch, round cake pans, *or* place parchment paper circles coated with flour in the bottom of the pans.

Beat butter until light and fluffy. Gradually add sugar, beating constantly until thoroughly mixed. Add yolks, one at a time, beating well after each addition. Sift flour with baking powder and salt. Add the dry ingredients to the butter mixture in two parts, alternating with buttermilk *or* coconut milk. Beat in the coconut extract and lemon zest.

In a separate mixing bowl, beat egg whites until medium-firm peaks form. Fold one third of the egg whites into the batter, then fold in the remaining whites.

Divide batter between the pans, and bake on the middle rack of the oven about 30 minutes. Cool in pans on a wire rack for 10 minutes. Remove from pans and finish cooling completely. Decorate with buttercream frosting.

Orange Buttercream Frosting
1 pound unsalted butter, at room temperature
16-ounce bag powdered sugar
4 teaspoons grated orange zest
orange food coloring

Whip butter and sugar together until perfectly smooth. Add grated zest one teaspoon at a time and blend well. Add orange food coloring one drop at a time until the desired shade is achieved.

RECIPES PROVIDED BY SHERRY GORE

Sherry Gore is the author of *An Amish Bride's Kitchen,* the editor of *Cooking and Such* magazine and *The Pinecraft Pauper,* and a contributing writer for the national edition of *The Budget.* She is a member of a Beachy Amish Mennonite church and makes her home in Sarasota with her family.

Sherry enjoys corresponding with reader friends everywhere. She can be contacted at www.SherryGoreBooks.com or via e-mail at TasteofPinecraft@gmail.com.

Acknowledgments

To Jeffry J. Bizon, MD, OB/GYN—Much like your patients, I rely on your expertise and on your tender, caring spirit. Whether you have been in the middle of a busy workday or enjoying downtime with your wonderful family or finishing another umpteen-mile run, you have always made time to answer my numerous questions, even before my first book was contracted. My gratitude to you and Kathy is deep.

To Rachel Esh, my energetic and good-humored Old Order Amish friend—I'm so grateful that you're open to my many questions, that you're willing to make time to return my calls, and that you own a dry goods store with a community phone! You keep showing up in my books because you are a fascinating and unique person. I hope you never change! Thank you for inviting me into your life.

To everyone at WaterBrook Multnomah, from marketing to sales to production to editorial—You are incredible!

To my expert in the Pennsylvania Dutch language, who wishes to remain anonymous—May an unexpected someone cross your path who gives as selflessly to you as you have to me.

About the Author

CINDY WOODSMALL is a *New York Times* best-selling author whose connection with the Amish community has been featured on *ABC Nightline,* in the *Wall Street Journal,* and in other media. She is the author of the Sisters of the Quilt series, *The Sound of Sleigh Bells,* and a nonfiction work, *Plain Wisdom: An Invitation into An Amish Home and the Hearts of Two Women,* which was written with her closest Old Order Amish friend. Cindy lives in Georgia with her family. Visit her Web site at CindyWoodsmall.com.

A rich and intricate tapestry of friends, love, faith, and family

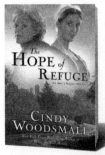

Two people from vastly different worlds. Can New Yorker Cara Moore and Amish man Ephraim Mast get past long-hidden secrets and find assurance in the midst of desperation?

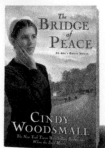

Lena and Grey have been lifelong friends, but their relationship begins to crumble amidst unsettling deceptions, propelling both of them to finally face their own secrets. Can they find a way past their losses and discover the strength to build a new bridge?

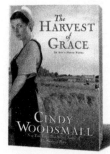

Fleeing a terrible mistake, Sylvia Fisher dedicates herself to saving the failing Blank farm. When prodigal son Aaron returns, he is surprised by this unusual farmhand who opposes all his plans.

Read an excerpt from these books and more on WaterBrookMultnomah.com!

Two friends from different worlds—
one **Old Order Amish**, one *Englischer* —
share the truths that bring them together.

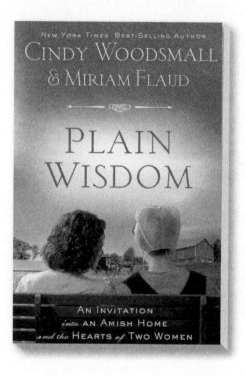

Best-selling author Cindy Woodsmall and Old Order Amish woman Miriam
Flaud's book, *Plain Wisdom,* celebrates the common ground found in
womanhood and the challenges of being wives and mothers. Cindy and
Miriam reveal how God has brought both of them through difficult
and enjoyable times as they each face life with grace and strength.

Read an excerpt from this book and more on
WaterBrookMultnomah.com!

The beautiful work of his hands may be just what Beth needs to find hope again.

CINDY WOODSMALL

New York Times Best-selling Author of *When the Soul Mends*

The SOUND of SLEIGH BELLS

A beautiful carving and a well-intentioned aunt just might thaw two frozen, lonely hearts and give them a second chance at love—just in time for Christmas.

Read an excerpt from this book and more on WaterBrookMultnomah.com!

Can Hannah find refuge, redemption, and a fresh beginning after her world is shattered?

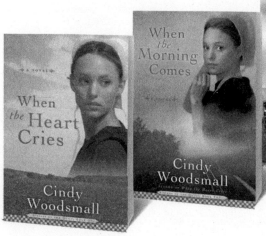

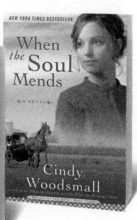

Also available in a 3-in-1 volume:

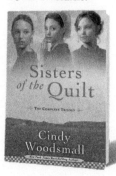

When Hannah Lapp, a simple 17-year-old Amish girl, finds her life shattered by one brutal act, she must face the rejection of family and friends and the questioning of her faith. Will she find her way back to the soul she fears may be lost forever?

Read an excerpt from these books and more on WaterBrookMultnomah.com!